A HANDFUL OF GHOSTS

'Thirteen: the obvious number for a
handful of ghostly tales, strange, weird,
spooky, supernatural tales. When I began
to collect these stories, writing to various
authors to ask whether they would send
me a ghost story, I really had no idea
what to expect. What, after all, is a ghost
story? Need it necessarily contain a
ghost? Perhaps a definition would be,
more accurately, a story in some way
connected with the supernatural, relating
an experience in some manner outside
this everyday world. And, sometimes,
the more conventional aspects of ghostly
stories: darkness, a fitful moon, owls
hooting, what else one will to induce a
shiver, may seem less strange than an
experience encountered in bright daylight,
beneath the sun . . . '

From the foreword by
Barbara Ker Wilson

About the compiler:

Barbara Ker Wilson was born in the north of England. At school, she devoted so much time and enthusiasm to editing the magazine that she subsequently failed most of her exams. She took up a career in publishing, joining the Oxford University Press in 1949 as a shorthand-typist. She has worked for a number of publishing companies in the UK and Australia, graduating from shorthand-typist through production and publicity departments to become eventually a managing editor for children's books. She went to live in Australia in 1964 and now lives in Melbourne, near the heart of the city, in an old terrace house with a view of slate roofs and chimneys. Barbara Ker Wilson has written a number of novels and non-fiction works for a wide age-range of young readers; her special interests are folklore and social history.

A Handful of Ghosts

Thirteen Eerie Tales by Australian Authors

Collected by
Barbara Ker Wilson

KNIGHT BOOKS
Hodder and Stoughton

Printed and bound in Great Britain for
Hodder and Stoughton Paperbacks, a
division of Hodder and Stoughton Ltd.,
Mill Road, Dunton Green, Sevenoaks,
Kent (Editorial Office: 47 Bedford
Square, London, WC1 3DP) by
Hunt Barnard Printing Ltd.,
Aylesbury, Bucks.

ISBN 0 340 24034 2

CONTENTS

Acknowledgment
THE GHOST OF GARTENSCHMUCK is an extract from
Chapter 8 of UNCLE GUSTAV'S GHOSTS by Colin Thiele,
published by Rigby Ltd, Adelaide, 1974.

FOREWORD

Thirteen: the obvious number for a handful of ghostly tales: eerie tales, strange, weird, spooky, supernatural tales. When I began to collect these stories, writing to various authors to ask whether they would send me a ghost story, I really had no idea what to expect. What, after all, is a ghost story? Need it necessarily contain a ghost? Perhaps a definition would be, more accurately, a story in some way connected with the supernatural, relating an experience in some manner outside this everyday world. And, sometimes, the more conventional aspects of ghostly stories: darkness, a fitful moon, owls hooting, what else one will to induce a shiver, may seem less strange than an experience encountered in bright daylight, beneath the sun. Just as a little ghost, gentle, light-footed, no more than a rustle of silk or a sigh, may seize hold of the imagination more effectively than any of your great galumphing ghosts carrying their heads under their arms, rattling chains, groaning and wailing.

It was exciting—and often surprising and intriguing—to receive the responses to my invitation. Every author I wrote to was Australian; their stories show a wide range of setting, from the Gippsland hills to New Guinea; from a deserted outback mine to an hotel in an English cathedral town. No fewer than five of the stories are based upon, or contain echoes of some happening which their authors have themselves experienced: inexplicable, haunting happenings now woven into the fabric of a story. Ivan Southall's FORTY-TWO STEPS LEFT; Nance Donkin's ROOM 409; my own story, with the background of a summer's day on Sark: these are three of the five. If one *has* a seemingly inexplicable tale to tell, it tumbles out of the mind very readily, as though the telling were needful, the experience something which demands to be shared ... for comfort, perhaps.

Then, what is the actual effect a ghostly story has upon one? Spine-chilling; intriguing; mystifying—it may be any of these, or all of them together. As a child, I recall two occasions when I was 'frightened to death' by reading ghost stories. Once, late at night, by myself in the family air-raid shelter, built at the end of the garden (for it was wartime) I pored over W.W. Jacob's incomparably sinister tale THE MONKEY'S PAW, with a shadow-casting kerosene lamp glowing softly beside the page, leaving the outer edges of the shelter, with its carpet of soft peat, cast in darkness. Yet, in retrospect, what delicious terror that was. And a very different sort of terror to that which one knew, concurrently, of planes, bombs, gunfire and falling shrapnel.

The other time was in a quiet room, so quiet, one sunny afternoon, alone in a house: there was a story, its details forgotten now, which conjured up such a powerful, convincing atmosphere that the only thing to do was to fling aside the book and run headlong outside into the orchard and stand in the fresh, mind-blowing breeze beneath the ancient apple-trees. (So, for me, the smell of a Cox's orange pippin is forever linked with the ghost of a ghost story.)

Here, then, are our thirteen Australian ghost stories—to read when you are by yourself, or maybe aloud, in company. There will be something here that lingers in the mind ... something passing strange.

Barbara Ker Wilson

A Handful of Ghosts

FORTY-TWO STEPS LEFT
Ivan Southall

It was 1950, or possibly 1951. I had a written record of it once, but it is lost. There are two documents I have lost in the last twenty years—the record of the event I am about to describe and a detailed account of a dream, one of the two or three striking dreams of my life. Everything I could recapture of that dream was written down first thing the "morning after"—about seven quarto pages, I think—but within a few days was lost, as if neither dream nor record of it had happened. I cannot now remember what the dream was about. A more recent dream is *not* forgotten, and day by day I wait for events to interpret it. When special things happen you are wise to accept them as special. If you attempt to ignore them you are denying one of the wonders of being human.

This story is not an account of a dream, however dream-like parts of it might appear to be. In it I am speaking as a person relating an actual incident, not as a story-teller. Inaccuracies of mood or language, if they occur, will be due only to the stretch of years and the misting of the edges that one cannot avoid. The event, how and where it took place and the questions arising from it, I vouch for.

We lived then in the Dandenong Ranges, three kilometres from the nearest township, fifty kilometres from Melbourne, having not long before decided that the city was not a suitable place for a poor and struggling writer to be. Every bit of money I could scrape together had gone into the purchasing of this place—a run-down, "failed farmlet" of about six hectares, several leaning outbuildings, and a low-grade shack with termites gnawing through foundations and walls. When I call it a "failed farmlet" that is exactly what I mean. As far as I have been able to learn no one had succeeded there: plain bad luck or notable misfortune or tragedy appeared to have overwhelmed every family who had called it home. I did not know that then, and I am certain we did not break the chain. Our sojourn there, a continuous adventure of something like thirteen years and thirteen weeks and thirteen days (if you care to express it that way) was filled with trauma and catastrophe.

It would have been well on into the evening, perhaps ten pm. We were in the front room, then lined with old smoke-stained plywood, the joins battened with pine, a messmate fire burning quietly in the hearth, a kerosene mantle lamp, with a shade like a Chinese hat, hanging from the ceiling and giving off a soft white light.

There were five of us—Richard and his wife, my wife and her mother, and myself, but whether five makes a number that invokes magic I cannot say. I hardly ever think about these things—numbers thirteen and seven and three and all that stuff. Perhaps black cats passed by outside, or owls sat on crooked poles, or the moon hid behind strangely-shaped clouds. You might know more about that kind of thing than I. There we were, seated round that table, with arms outstretched, forefingers resting on the base of an upturned drinking glass, the fifth person ready with pencil in hand to record any messages that might come through.

"They can't be serious," I thought. "How can they play it with faces so straight? Messages through a drinking glass? Spirits of the dead coming into my living-room to move a common old tumbler? It's beneath the dignity of spirits—if there be such things as spirits anywhere."

I was troubled by the clumsiness of the procedure, by a lack of what I could have termed "a proper respect". The whole thing had an artificial feeling, as if it were being "cooked up" to entertain idle people. An upended drinking glass in the midst of a circle of twenty-six letters and ten figures on my own table top—A to Z and 1 to 0, the word YES at the head of the table and NO at the foot, as if it were a parlour game, something like roulette. All those little pieces of paper that we could displace too easily with our sleeves or with a heavily-expelled breath! Spirits moving a common old tumbler and spelling out messages on a polished table-top!

There sat Richard repeating his question in a low voice. "Is anyone there? Is anyone there? If so, please move the glass to YES."

Again and again he addressed the question—but to what? Was one reasonably expected to believe that spirits were forever drifting about, like spiders in dark cupboards, waiting for people with upended drinking glasses to ask silly questions? The spirits made it clear that they were not. The glass remained as it was, supremely unmoving, supremely *put*.

"I have seen it work often," my mother-in-law said. "Home in England we used to do it a lot. Sunday night after tea. It was all the rage twenty years back."

"Is anyone there? Is anyone there?"

"I don't like it," my wife said. "I don't want spirits brought in here. What'll happen when I'm here on my own at night? Are they going to come back then? What sort of spirits are they, anyway? I don't want a haunted house."

"There's nothing to fear," Richard said. "They only come through the glass. They like to have a talk. They won't come at all unless you invite them in."

"That's stupid," my wife said.

"The pioneers used to do it," Richard said, almost too

patiently, "when they needed help or medical advice or an expert opinion. They'd ask the glass what to do and in a while they'd get the answer."

"You can't expect anyone to believe that," I said.

"But it's true. I've spoken to old people about it. If they were desperate and didn't know what to do, they'd ask the glass. When they ran out of their own ideas and the need was great, they'd ask the glass. And back would come the answer. True ... Is anyone there? Come on, Mr Glass; is anyone there?"

"I think it's all wrong," I said. "I don't think we should be doing it. It's like a seance."

"It *is* a seance."

"I've always been warned that you shouldn't do this sort of thing. There's no saying what you're going to call up. You might get on to an evil spirit or something."

"Oh, come on, Southall; you're not going to tell me you believe that."

"I don't know whether I believe it or whether I don't. But you believe it, don't you? You set it all up, didn't you? It was your idea. Surely you didn't go to all this trouble expecting it not to happen?"

So the glass moved.

That glass tugged as if a hand had been inserted inside it through the base of the table and off it moved unevenly, as if reluctant to slide, across the table to YES.

There we sat, for the moment aghast, for the moment breathless, eyeing each other off.

"You did it, Richard, didn't you?"

"No, no, I swear it."

"You did it, Mum, didn't you?"

"No. Truly, I didn't.

"You did it, Ivan."

"I did nothing of the kind."

"You must have done," Richard said, accusing me, "just to make a monkey of me."

14

"I didn't!"

Richard, I think, was beginning to look nervously into the shadows of the room. "Someone must be there then?"

"Yes. It looks like it."

"It's never worked for me before."

"I thought you were the expert."

"No, no. It's never worked for me. Never. Ever. Not *properly*. You muck about, you know; you give it a push. Somebody *must* have done it."

No one would accept that kind of blame. Everyone said NO.

Richard drew a heavy breath. "All right," he said, "is anyone there? Really and truly there?"

Off the glass moved, around the table, inside the letters and the figures, like a runner inside the rails, and stopped again at YES.

Everyone sighed. Everyone thought about it. My wife— with the pencil in her hand—became agitated.

Richard said, "Will you please spell your name?"

The glass at once moved with purpose and force, from letter to letter, back and forth across the table, and long before it finished I knew what was happening. The name coming off that table was that of my father, dead at that time for fifteen years: he died when I was a boy.

I took my hand away and shook my head vigorously. "No, no. I don't believe it."

"You've got to believe it."

"I don't see that I have to believe anything. Someone here is not being fair and I think it's in very bad taste."

Richard said, "Who knows anything about Ivan's father? I don't. Does anyone else? They don't, you know. No one knows a thing about your father except you. Question the glass. Find out."

"I don't believe my father would move a glass. He was a religious man."

"What's that got to do with it?"

15

"Move a glass? It's like a parlour trick. It's like a guessing game. There's no dignity in it. It's not even a proper seance—and I'd not be believing in it if it were a proper seance."

"Ask it some questions," Richard insisted. "Go on. It can't hurt you."

"I don't want to."

"You're not being a very good sport, are you?"

"It's not your father, it's my father. How would you feel?"

"I don't know how I'd feel. My father's not dead. Ask him when he was born or something?"

I sat a while and thought it over, and my wife was shaking her head, but perhaps we were taking it too seriously, and perhaps *I* was not being "gracious" to my guests. I was practically picking a fight with them. All right—if I questioned it and it answered incorrectly, that would be the end of it. It was as simple as that. So I asked, "When were you born?"

The glass spelt out, "*1888*".

"Is that right?" Richard said.

Yes, it was right.

"Well, ask it some more."

"When did you die?"

"*1935*."

That answer, too, was right.

"What day did you die?"

"*Saturday: December 14th.*"

Right again—as was the answer to every personal question I put. I am unable to recall now, with certainty, my eventual state of mind, but I remember a growing awe, a feeling that this was an exceptional experience no matter *what* the experience actually was. I realized it could have been a form of self-delusion or self-hypnosis. After all, things like that could happen, and one person present *did* know the answer to all the questions and that was myself. I

16

could have been moving the glass myself—though I would have sworn it was not the case.

Richard urged for a change of tactics. He was nervous and intrigued and apparently experiencing my own kind of doubts. "Ask different sorts of questions—things you have no knowledge of. Ask about the future."

But I was reluctant to do this; already there was a possibility that this incredible incident was truly happening, and in a way it was good to think that it was. If it *were* my father, it proved the reality of life after death, and no matter how often other people might present "proof" of this kind, there is nothing as satisfying as having your very special own. So had we, in fact, already taken it far enough? Was one being *greedy* to press on? Or was one foolish not to? Or would the posing of questions about the "future" be a silly thing to do? I lived then—as now—on the understanding that tomorrow belongs to tomorrow, and tomorrow, particularly for a poor writer, may be even worse than today. The Australian writer, back when I started out, lived from hand to mouth, without grants or subsidies or patronage. It was a case of *survive*, somehow, from day to day. Perhaps it was better not to know *anything* about tomorrow. I compromised, and said, "I wasn't a good pilot at first. I had a lot to learn when I got on to operations. How is it that I survived the war—when every day I was sure I couldn't last?"

There was a pause, then the glass spelt out a disturbing message. "*I flew beside you.*"

This disconcerted me. What sort of mystery was it, that was developing under our hands? What kind of *influence* was talking to us?

If I, unwittingly, were pushing the glass myself, would I have answered my own question in that way? Would anyone present at the table have produced a response of that kind? I am sure no one would have dared.

I said, "I'm trying to be a writer. I suppose you know

that. Is it worth my while pressing on? Am I going to make the grade?"

"*Yes. Have faith.*"

Where was I to go from there? What was I to believe? For some reason I cannot explain, I then stepped outside of my own character and asked the type of question that did not fit me then any more than it fits me now. (I do not *want* to know these things.) I said, "What will I be doing in a month?"

"Digging for gold."

I was suddenly irritated with myself and with everything else; suddenly disappointed that an exciting experience could degenerate to the level of a treasure hunt. "The whole thing's stupid," I said. "My father didn't care about gold and I don't care about gold. I'm not going on with it. It's phoney."

But the glass itself went on. I had no further say over it. Went on and on and on. There was gold, the glass said, sixty thousand pounds worth (probably half-a-million dollars in the values of today) at a depth of twenty metres, at the bottom of a shaft sunk sixty years before by Chinese prospectors who had died by misadventure. (One might have murdered the other out of greed, but I am not sure if murder came into the events of that night. I might have invented the murder when I came to write *The Fox Hole* about fifteen years later.) If, the glass said, I would proceed along a given compass-bearing for a given distance—a considerable distance, something like three hundred metres—then turn left at right-angles for a farther distance of forty-two steps, the shaft and the gold would be mine.

There the "seance" ended. It was late at night, and in every way we had had enough, but as soon as I moved away from the table I stopped believing. Although outside my understanding, I was convinced the whole thing was an illusion. Somehow or other we had been set up, but by what agency or influence? Look for gold? Hunt for a shaft?

18

Not in a lifetime. Not only would I not look for a shaft, I would not allow any tumbler to be turned upside-down on my table-top for that purpose again.

Next morning, at about six, my mother-in-law was on the move. "Come along," she said, "everybody out. Let's find it."

I protested. No one in his right mind, I said, could fall for a thing like that. Nor was it a case of stepping outside and simply pacing off the distance. It was not something you could settle in five minutes to humour a whim. I knew that the starting position given and the compass-bearing stated would send us off through dense blackberry-infested bush that had not been disturbed in many years. It could take hours. And for what?

"For sixty thousand pounds worth of gold. Isn't it worth a day of your time?"

"I don't know that it is."

"If you let it pass," my mother-in-law said, "it will worry you for the rest of your life."

"I'm sure it won't. It's not the sort of thing that would worry me for the rest of the day."

"Look at it carefully," she said. "Was it your father? Was it real? Was it false? Aren't those questions worth answering?"

I accepted the argument. Perhaps it was destined that I should, though I am by no means certain about "destiny"; neither certain that it is lying in wait for us, nor certain that it is not.

After breakfast we set off with surveyor's tape, compass, blackberry slasher and axe, and as I had suspected we were soon hacking into dense bush, cutting through blackberry canes running wild and rampant, six metres long and very thick. It took several hours of hard and persistent

19

work to bring us accurately to the point where we were to turn at right-angles and proceed to the left. Richard and his wife had gone by then, back to Melbourne I would think, precisely why I cannot remember, but I *do* know that by then only three adults remained, my wife, her mother, and myself. We were in old bush, in a deep gully, with trees so thick and tall and undergrowth so vigorous that no sunshine reached us, only shadow and shade and dampness. There was the sound of a bubbling creek, as if water were running over rocks or spilling into a pit. There were bellbirds and whipbirds and tiny scrub thornbills. Blackberries were cruel and thick. I cannot explain why I had not long before then given up in futility and disgust.

"Forty-two steps to the left," I said, and passed the anchor end of the tape to my wife. "Don't let go of it. Hold on tight. I'll pace out the distance." But it was not to be as easy as that. I became caught up in blackberries and dogwood scrub again and had to cut my way through with the axe. At about ten metres I climbed a mound, and was already out of sight of my wife. But I climbed that mound, perhaps two metres high and three across, with something like wonderment. It was obvious that the mound was man-made of soil brought up from a depth. It was of grey rock and hungry grey dirt, though every other cubic metre of earth round about was rich and red and of volcanic origin. At the foot of the mound, with the tape running out past twelve metres, criss-crossed by blackberries and a few rotten logs, framed by timbers encrusted with fungi, brimming with water, was the shaft.

I stared at it, overwhelmed, apparently unable to hear the calls of my wife: "Are you all right? Why don't you answer us?"

"It's here," I said.

And it was.

Even the families who pioneered the district in the early 1900's had no knowledge of a shaft in that position. Even the prospectors who panned the gully creek in the Great Depression of the 1930's had not found it.

There was our shaft, our secret shaft, which we plumbed to a depth of over twelve metres before we ran out of pipes to screw together. There was our shaft with a quantity of "ore" spilled at the top, ore that I crushed on an anvil with a hammer, ore that showed the colour of gold, though the sample, like the record of the event written at the time, is lost.

Sixty thousand pounds worth of gold? Was it really there? How far down? How much water to pump away? What else might we find? What else might occur? Register a claim and start a gold rush? See that beautiful gully (with lyrebirds downstream) again torn apart? Sixty thousand pounds worth of gold. A fortune in those days. Economic security for life. No need to grow food to feed the family. No need to live in a shack. No need to work as a labourer (or was it as a slave?) for fourteen hours straight starting at 1.45 am three nights of the week. No conflict over whether or not I should go on struggling to write. Sixty thousand pounds worth of gold—the easy way out.

I don't know what happened that night with our half-baked seance. I don't know what spoke to me through the glass. But I was given a choice—a life of struggle as a writer, alone, against the great odds that all writers of serious intent eventually confront—or the easy way out.

I decided for the struggle.

I could not find that place, now, to save my life. Nor could anyone else. I have forgotten the compass bearing, I have forgotten the distance, and bulldozers have been through and changed the face of the earth.

THE TRAIN FROM MOONDYKE
James Menzies

"That's where the train from Moondyke used to come in," the old man had said, pointing out of the window at what seemed to be an area of virgin bushland. He had been sitting in front of me in a first-class carriage of the express—and at once I'd looked out too, caught by something in the tone of his voice: as if, perhaps, there was an odd little story to tell about the Moondyke train. But all I had seen was a small station as we rushed through it. Pine Hill Junction it was called—though I'd noticed no junction there. Perhaps had I been younger than my eighteen years, and more impulsive—or older, and less proud of travelling first-class, incognito—I would have asked the old gentleman the meaning of Moondyke and its train. Was it long ago? Was there anything interesting about it? And probably he'd have answered *no*. Whereupon, in a few kilometres, I must have ceased to think of it.

But I had not spoken.

Years later, when I happened to be within travelling distance of the Pine Hill area, and had a clear day ahead of me, I decided to drive there. I realized that I was seeking out that name, Moondyke—and reflected that a touch of mystery had certainly stayed in my mind, or I'd not be bothering to make such an excursion. I wondered idly if I would regret it.

Walking was always a pleasure to me, particularly if there was some ruin at the end of a tour, or relics along the way. Here I had vague ideas of following the old railway line. I took a detailed map sheet of the area, and drove first to Pine Hill Junction. The place was deserted, no one dwelt nearby; but I did find the formation of a branch line, leading off into the bush, not far from the present station. I followed a road in the same direction and in less than a mile came to Pine Hill itself. A dozen houses, a sawmill, a huge old hotel, and many remains of earlier buildings—all strung out over a considerable distance down a wide main street.

I went through the town to the ruins of a large mineral treatment works, built on the side of a low hill above a river. I could see where there had once been a substantial bridge crossing the river. I looked at the map. From Pine Hill the mineral railway had run out quite a long way, to the mines at Moondyke. It traversed some difficult country, as far as railway construction was concerned, and yet seemed to be the only route that could have been taken. The map showed the line marked simply as "abandoned". The mines at the end of it, on the steep side of the Moondyke Range, were also shown as abandoned. Directly below the principal mine was an upper part of the same river that flowed through Pine Hill. There it occupied a gorge, above which, on the opposite side, was a winding road that came within three kilometres of the mine in a straight line—the nearest access to it.

I got out of the car to have a look at the treatment-plant· site. As I went in, I became aware that someone else was moving along an old pathway above me, back toward the road. A girl: she had been watching me, I thought. We exchanged glances. I smiled, but there was no response

23

from her. She turned towards the town, and I stood regarding her a moment: dusty riding boots, jeans, a straw hat. I shrugged my shoulders.

Below, there was a battered utility truck parked, and I could see a man working. I went down to him; and found that he was quite willing to stop work and talk. He'd been pulling up a length of copper wire from beneath the ground, digging with a shovel, and moving slabs of concrete and heavy pieces of timber out of the way with a crowbar. It was a hot windless day. I didn't envy him his job.

He explained the copper wire. "Runs from that brick place over there to the old power house," he said. "Worth a few bob—if I ever get it up; see, it's very thick! What are you doing—just having a look about?"

"Yes. I'd hoped to get up to the Moondyke mine, and the old railway there. Do you know if one can walk in from that road across the gorge?"

"You can. But it's quite a walk, down and up. There's a ford at the river—be an easy crossing now, the water's low."

We smoked and talked; reflectively on his part, patiently on mine—yet I heard what I wished to know, and rather more than I'd imagined. He spoke about the mines, and the trouble they'd had. "The railway was put through in the time of the first company," he said. "I think building it was one of the main reasons they went broke. Then another company took over—all this is long ago of course—and they did well for a while, and struggled on for a good many more years. It was a big concern at its best time: you can see by looking round here."

"What did they have up at the mine?"

"Just a crushing plant, I think. Or maybe not even that. Lots of people up there once—in its heyday."

"How long was the line?"

"Fifty kilometres. Narrow gauge."

"Was it? I thought it joined the main line?"

"No, a branch ran off from the main line just as far as the works here."

"Oh. Is there anything left, along the way to Moondyke?"

He nodded. "Rails are still there; couldn't get things out very easily, after the bridge was gone."

We looked down at the river.

"Did it get washed away in a flood?"

"What was left of it. That's where the train went in."

"Into the river? What happened?"

"An engine with about twenty ore trucks crashed through the bridge. Some say it was going too fast; others reckon the old bridge was rotten anyway. Of course, the engine could have broken an axle or something as it was going on to the bridge. There used to be two locos—both secondhand when they came here, I believe. Towards the end, when the company was about to fold up, things were pretty free and easy; the driver and fireman on the engine that crashed used to try to set a record each trip down from Moondyke. They say they used to do the trip faster than the other engine, which was a bigger one. You can imagine it: tight curves and grades steep as hell in some places, no brakes on the wagons. Of course, there's a few long straight sections too—down on the flat. They even had the engine rigged to run on a higher boiler pressure than it should have. They say the guard was scared of it, and sometimes wouldn't go with them—he'd leave earlier on a horse, ride through to the river here, and walk over the bridge and wait for the train! Anyhow, the driver and fireman both got killed. Must have hit the river at a hell of a speed ..."

He told me that the line ran straight for several miles approaching the bridge, then pointed to where it had continued straight for a little way past the bridge, before curving right around to climb up to the ore-dump on the hillside above us. "You can see the wreck of the engine and some of the wagons when the river gets really low," he said. "Soon after the crash, there was a big flood—took the rest of the bridge; it wasn't worth fixing things up again. The company finished then. They talked of putting a cableway across the gorge to that road, but didn't do anything. The last few hundred tonnes of ore are still sitting up at the mine."

"What happened to the other loco?"

"The old No 1? She's still out there."

"What, at the mine?"

"Supposed to be there somewhere. Didn't see it myself, although I've only been up to the place once, and didn't stay long. One fellow here in town used to say that they pushed it inside the main adit of the mine, and blocked the entrance: it *is* all fallen in. You reckon you'll get up to the mines, eh?"

I smiled. "I'll try."

"I met a fellow once who'd been walking along the valley, camped there overnight somewhere, and he told us he'd heard an engine during the night. Insisted on it. Reasonable sort of a fellow, too. 'Course it must have been a train way out on the main line. There are still a few steamers that go through occasionally. Marvellous how sound travels on a quiet night."

At last my informant went back to work on his piece of buried copper. I was about to leave him, to look over the old works, when I remembered the girl I'd seen. "Who was that girl, here?" I asked.

"Dunno her name. Comes now and then and stays with the people who have the pub. Relatives of hers. Often see her wandering about. Bit of a dreamer, I think; something a bit odd about her. A few months back, last time she was here, I was working over near the old furnace—see it there?—I happened to look up, and there she was, up on the catwalk, just standing, looking out. She beckoned me to come up—and I did. It was about dusk. She pointed away

26

up the valley: at a light there, a long way off. 'Look!' she said; 'Can you see it?' I said yes: hikers, or someone camping, I guessed. And she went on, 'It's a very bright light—being so far away.' I told her: 'It's probably one of those pressure lamps—they're as bright as that.' She shook her head: 'It moved.' Why not? I answered; you can carry 'em around! She wouldn't say any more to me after that. Bit funny, she is . . ."

After I'd walked through the remains of the treatment works I went down to the river bank. A pretty spot—especially after the litter of broken concrete and rusty ironwork in the area above. I could see where the old Moondyke line ran out across the plain towards the mountains; though I could not see the actual beginning of it, for there was a huge willow-tree now overhanging the farther abutment of the bridge. I was intrigued to learn that the line apparently had been left intact, not having thought it would be so inaccessible.

I went back to the town, and into the bar of the hotel. There were several local men drinking, and a woman behind the counter talking to them. They didn't take much notice of me. Soon the girl I had seen earlier came in and took over the barmaid's duties. And a little later, when the men left, the bar became silent. I thought the girl might wonder if I'd learnt anything of her from the man at the old treatment plant. I glanced cautiously at her: a face that showed a slight reserve, a suspicion—except once, in an unguarded moment that I caught, when her eyes held a calm expression: an appraisal of me that was touched with amusement. I considered making some reference to the light in the valley: an honest, simple inquiry. But I could see that I was really in no position to be the one to speak of it first.

"Do you serve lunch here?" I asked.

"Yes. Do you want some?"

"Thank you."

She went out to the kitchen, and returned.

I remarked, "This afternoon I'm going up to the old Moondyke mine, if I can get there. What's the road like, do you know?"

"Oh, quite trafficable."

"Have you ever been to the mine?"

"No." She looked at me briefly, with some expectancy, with a little release of confidence: I was just that much less of a stranger. When I said nothing, however, she turned away, and moved along to the other end of the bar.

I sat down to lunch; and found that the waitress was the same girl. I was the only person in the dining-room.. Her manner was again detached, rather impersonal: I wondered over ways of satisfactorily changing that, but my meal passed in silence.

As I was about to leave the table she spoke. "It's dangerous ..., up around the mine, they say. And going there alone."

I smiled. "Would you like to come?"

"No, thank you. I didn't mean that."

An automatic reply—but a slight frown came to her face: "Just thought I ought to be careful?"

"Yes," she said.

I followed the narrow gravel road for more than thirty kilometres before I saw anything of the old line, away across the valley. There was a short section of the formation visible, high up on the steep side of the range: it came from a fold between hills, ran along a narrow ledge, and disappeared into a cutting in a spur. As I went on there were several more stretches of the railway to be seen; I stopped to look at them, and identified each on my map. Finally I caught sight of the mine, its long mullock heaps streaming down into the valley.

I left the car, and clambered down to the river easily enough; the crossing was wide, but the water only up to my knees. I had a long slow job getting up to the mine, though. I thought that mountainside must go upwards for ever! For the last half-hour I climbed upon loose broken rock that continually gave way beneath my feet: I could hear lumps of rock tumbling down behind me—some, it seemed, surely going right to the river.

There was nothing much at the mine. Other people had been there, over the years. The entrances of the various adits into the mountain were all blocked with rockfalls; a lot of the old equipment had been pushed over the edge, and lay strewn below. There were several levels, each with a narrow horizontal path around the slope, the lowest one being that of the railway. I followed it along.

There was no sign of an engine, nor even of any of the ore trucks. The rails and sleepers lay untouched, however; and a row of telephone poles, with some wires still trailing from them, ran alongside the track into a cutting ahead. I'd seen a few of the same poles back near town, just over the river: I thought, fifty kilometres to go!

I decided to explore for a little while, down the track. Soon I came to a small flat area, from which a rocky gully dropped steeply down to the river on one side, and on the other a broad little valley, turning quickly into a ravine, ran up through the mountain. Here there were old huts and sheds, a large water tank, evidently fed from a dam farther up, and railway sidings arranged in the shape of a Y, so that trains could be turned round. On one siding stood some dilapidated wooden ore trucks and a van. Fruit trees grew here and there; and in front of one ruined hut there were a few rose bushes. So much for the settlement of Moondyke, I mused, looking at it a trifle sadly.

The map showed a tunnel on the line a short distance ahead, and I thought I would have time to get that far and return by dark. There was a noticeable downward gradient as I walked, but it was not easy going; in some places young trees had grown up between the sleepers; there'd been a landslide in another place, leaving the track barely supported. I came to the tunnel. It ran in a curve, beneath the towering ridge of a spur; its length was only about a hundred metres, and I got through with only an occasional stumble. The line came out on to a ledge of solid rock, from which there was a magnificent view of the valley away towards Pine Hill. Impressed with this panorama I kept walking ... Once or twice I thought of the girl at the hotel; sometimes I wondered if I might find the old steam engine, rusting away, sitting on the track in some unvisited place.

Suddenly I realized that it would probably be nightfall before I got back to the car. I turned at once, and began to hurry—running, where it was safe to do so. If I could at least get down to the river by dark, I thought ...

It seemed to take ages even before the tunnel came into sight. At dusk it was still hot and sultry; I wished I'd brought something to drink. With the prospect of a hurried and less pleasant return trip the old railway began to lose some of its interest. The mouth of the tunnel was black, unfriendly. I did not feel like entering it. However, to scramble over the top would be a hard climb and a waste of the now precious daylight. I went into the tunnel, carrying a stick to trail along the wall so that I might keep a regular path. But in spite of my precautions, I tripped on something between the rails. I fell—my hands touching nothing when I put them out to protect myself.

I sat up, dazed, a little mystified. It was darker than I'd realized in the middle of that confounded tunnel. The only thing I could see in such an intense blackness was the luminous dial of my watch. It said half-past eight. I could not remember what time it was when I'd come to the tunnel; but it seemed that an unreasonable amount of time had elapsed since then. The darkness was incredible—not the slightest glimmering anywhere. One hand was hurting where I'd cut it on something. I felt a rail beneath me, and the inside edge of it was sharp at the lower part of the head—like a rail frequently used, where the metal would be sharpened by the flanges of the wheels. I lit a match. Not only were the rails sharp-edged, but the tops of them were shining in the small yellow light. I couldn't account for it at all.

There was no way of telling which direction I had been going—I could not remember how the curve of the tunnel lay. I set off groping, stumbling, and eventually saw a lighter patch in front of me; then at last the dark sky of stars. Fortunately, I'd come out at the right end.

I stopped to examine the line again. Sure enough, it had the appearance of being in use regularly.

Away ahead, just for a moment, I saw a twinkling light through the trees on the mountainside. Had someone come in search of me, I wondered? I couldn't believe it. The light was perhaps from some other visitor to the mine. Though that too seemed doubtful. The light appeared to be closer than the Moondyke mine.

I walked on, whistling a tune softly in the clear still evening. Any annoyance was cancelled out by the puzzle of the rails, and of that light. I determined to be cheerful about it, nonetheless. When I got back to the car, relieved, comfortable there, I would have intriguing matters to think about indeed! I might even come up again tomorrow.

The rails continued in their thin shiny lines before me: I simply couldn't understand how I'd missed seeing in daylight the recent wear on them. Perhaps someone had been there with a trolley, running up and down. Though it was not a likely place for children's games ...

I saw the light again: close, this time. Then came

something that really startled me. *I heard faintly the unmistakable sound of an engine with steam up.*

At once I forgot my preoccupation with the railway line itself. How could there possibly be a locomotive nearby—and in going order? Where had it been hidden? I walked more slowly, and cautiously approached the sidings at the old Moondyke settlement. I'd seen every part of the track still existing; I was sure of that. There was nowhere at the mine, no hiding-place in the valley behind the settlement, where it could have been.

As the sound of the waiting engine grew louder I moved off the line itself, pausing every few metres to listen carefully. A powerful light showed the track now clear of any trees, with the rails shining distinctly. I scrambled through the bush, over a rocky slope, until I was adjacent to the sidings. I could see the engine. It stood at the head of the row of empty trucks and the van—a reasonable yet unbelievable spectacle.

I crept a little closer. It was, in fact, an alarming sight. The engine outlined against the night sky, an unfamiliar intruder, now—having suddenly appeared in this remote place without any of the warning sounds of its motion. I stared at it. An engine small by later standards, but typical of the heavier goods locomotives in use during the eighties; it showed the influence of American design of its period, in the large smokestack and the enormous lamp mounted high in front.

For a while, being both fearful of what I saw and fascinated by it, I stood securely in the bush shadows and watched. Nothing happened. There seemed to be no one about. The engine was still and quiet, apart from the sound of escaping steam, and a slight rumbling noise within itself. It looked harmless. It was simply waiting there ready to take the train down to Pine Hill!

With a rising courage I began moving towards the engine. I went up close, and felt the warmth of it. On the side of the cabin was a rivetted plate bearing the inscription 'No 1'. There was no one aboard.

I walked back alongside the train to the van. Its door was open, and inside there was a lamp burning. I climbed in, to look more closely. On the floor were some wooden crates, a mailbag, and an empty milk can. I was examining these items when I heard a deep-toned whistle from the engine.

At the same moment there was a violent jerk—I was thrown off-balance, and the door slid shut from the sudden movement of the van. The milk can fell over—rolling across the floor and back, as I jumped to the door and grabbed its handle. The handle was stiff and difficult to turn; the door seemed jammed hard. I got it open very slowly—the train meanwhile gaining speed, clattering across several sets of points: there was a thundering sound of the driving wheels slipping, a pause, as the throttle was cut, and the engineer caught traction again; and we moved away, ever faster. The door came open—but already we were travelling too quickly for me to risk jumping out into the darkness. I stood in the doorway, looking ahead, wondering whatever I could do.

The beat of the engine increased still more, and steadied at an alarmingly fast pace. We passed over the spot where the landslide had been without any trouble. (I couldn't remember having noticed it on my return walk: perhaps it was not as close to the track as I imagined.) But I could think of no way to get safely off the train—unless I could reach the engine, perhaps.

I climbed out on to the narrow footboard that ran along the side of the van, hanging tightly to the handrail—a procedure that scared me so much at first that I wished I'd jumped off the train earlier, regardless of what had happened. Fortunately I'd only gone several steps when the note of the engine changed, as it was swallowed up by the tunnel. I jumped back inside with a couple of seconds to spare. There was a burst of shattering noise, and clouds of grey smoke came into the van. The milk can rolled out

3

through the doorway, hit the wall of the tunnel, and was thrown back hard against the doorpost and bounced inside again. I put it in a corner, with the wooden crates around it. And I sat down on a seat below the swinging kerosene lamp.

In a moment we were on the ledge beyond the tunnel: flying round the side of a cliff, it seemed. The downhill grade was less pronounced for a time, and the driver increased his speed a little: the wheels screeched on the rails, a high-pitched frightening sound, and the old van jumped and groaned around each curve. I sat shaking, imagining myself and the van tumbling down the mountainside into the river.

I took the folded map from my pocket and peered at it in the unsteady light. There was another tunnel, some distance onwards. I traced the course of the railway: high over the valley as far as the second tunnel, then a twisting descent through the foothills, to the long straights and sweeping curves on the plain. Several creek crossings were shown on the flat country: I wondered if there were any washaways along the line ... We lurched round a sharp bend; the van shuddered and leapt as the wheels hit something—a rail out of joint; I would have to get to the engine!

I made my way with some trouble to the first wagon; and then with less difficulty moved from one wagon to the next—fully resolved to take charge of the engine now, and slow it down. As I advanced the wagons rattled and jumped and hopped about beneath me; a sudden lurching nearly sent me down between the second and third one back from the engine. Feeling very apprehensive again, I continued—and reached the tender at last. It was heaped with coal, above which there came periodically a red glow as the firebox door was opened. Obviously I had at least one person to deal with.

I stood on the front of the foremost wagon, clutching at

the top edge of the tender—and my feet and hands seemed likely to go in different directions, before I managed to haul myself up, to lie flat on the coal. I could not see who was in the cabin. Even when the little door was opened for another shovelful of coal, I could tell only that a dark shape, briefly silhouetted, was moving about down there. I shouted—and nothing happened. I began to crawl nearer, over the coal. Suddenly I was struck hard on the shoulder with the end of a fire-iron: they meant to knock me off the tender! I hastened back, puzzled and rather angry. I watched for a few minutes. The fire door opened and closed; there were the motions of a man wiping his face with a rag; a match flared up on one side of the cabin, and I saw the white dial of a pocket-watch illuminated. I shouted again; and there was no reaction from them. I picked up a good-sized lump of coal and prepared once more to descend the heap—but after receiving another swipe with the iron bar I retreated. I had an idea that I might be able to smash the water-level gauge: a tube of glass, above the firebox door. I threw lumps of coal as fast as I could—and in a moment they began to return, faster and more accurately: the engine crew had every advantage over myself, perched up on the coal heap.

Remembering the tunnel, and my dangerous position— apart from the flying coal—I jumped back into the wagon behind the tender. There appeared to be nothing I could do. I had no weapons to use against them, there were no air brakes to tamper with. I sat down in the wagon feeling quite helpless.

The tunnel brought smoke and cinders swirling around me as I crouched there with a handkerchief over my face. In another few minutes we were on a steeper downhill run. The train thundered along, the wheels shrilling loudly; the wagons rocked and jerked about. I could see the tender above me wildly swaying—every now and then producing a stunning bang as the wheels hit some bad joint in the rails.

I looked over the side of the wagon, to see a long sharp curve through a cutting just ahead—and it was taken at the same speed: the train, it seemed, about to roll into the outside bank any moment.

Incredibly, we stayed on the track. Soon the hills were left behind, and we were on the plain with its long straight stretches. I listened as the driver got a little more speed from his engine.

I thought of something which I should have tried earlier: to uncouple the wagons. It might still be possible. I leaned over the front end of the wagon I was in; but could see nothing in the darkness there. I wished I'd taken more notice of what the couplings were like. I thought of the lamp, back in the van. And I returned to the end of the train, jumping recklessly from wagon to wagon—in a way that I knew would cause me to shudder, later, if I survived!

I got the lamp, and the wind blew it out at once. I could see that it was futile to relight it. Leaning over the last wagon, I felt around in the space between it and the next one. My mind was blurred with the rushing thundering sound in my ears, and strangely lulled by the regular rapid clicking of the wheels over the rail-joints below. I found the coupling—but it was tight, as they all would be. I pulled at it vainly—hardly aware of what I was doing. I knew that I'd have to wait for a sudden slackening of speed. Even then, I'd have to be quick. I kept one hand on the coupling-link, ready, hopefully. But its tension never varied.

At last I abandoned the idea. I stood up again, hanging on to the edge of the wagon, looking out ahead. It was the river that had been worrying me, I realized. Whether the bridge was there or not, I was sure we had no chance of getting safely across it. The engine pounded on as fast as ever, a column of steam rising from it, swept back with the grey smoke. That fireman had certainly done a good job.

I felt myself beginning to sway. It was difficult to keep standing—not just because of the train's motion, any more.

I was terribly tired. Suddenly, there was a lessening of sound: the whole noise of the train dying in a few seconds. I had a glimpse of a large willow tree: one of its trailing branches hit me across the face.

I awoke to bright warm sunshine. Familiar noises nearby, birds calling, the soft lapping and gurgling of river water. A calm sky; another hot day. I was still weary, despite my sleep. I was aching all over, and damp to the skin. I couldn't remember the reason for it—but it was clear at once that I'd been swimming in the river with my clothes on. I noticed that I was on the same side as the town; just below the old treatment works, in fact. A pretty spot, the water cool and restful, the grassy bank firm beneath me. Why, I wondered, was I so bruised and dirty—so covered with cuts and scratches and black marks? I could see a willow-tree up on the opposite bank; below, there were several pieces of heavy timber stuck in the water: the remains of a bridge. An old railway line. Ah yes! Abandoned, the map had said.

Then, to my surprise, I found another person sitting close beside me. A girl wearing jeans, and a shady straw hat.

"You seemed to be all right," she said. "So I left you to sleep."

I just looked at her. She had freckles around her nose, and light green eyes. I wondered what her name was.

"How *do* you feel?" she asked.

"I think I need some breakfast."

She smiled. I hadn't seen her smile, before.

We walked to the hotel. On the way, I remarked that I had come from Moondyke; though I did not say *how*. She asked no questions—which soon brought me to ponder further over her. Later, I decided, when I had eaten and had a bath, I would get her to talk.

The woman was in the bar, with several customers. The publican soon appeared there too. And this time they certainly gave me their attention. I told them what I had done, where I had been, as far as the point where I'd fallen over in the tunnel. Presumably I had hit my head: they decided that I must have come to, dazed, perhaps having lost my memory temporarily—and not known where I was. Thus, it was quite logical that I'd set off following the old railway track, and, by mistake, had simply gone the opposite way from where I'd left my car. The girl smiled encouragingly at me, as this story developed.

But they remained incredulous. It was just not possible to walk over forty kilometres on a broken and overgrown track, in the dark, and to do it in the time that I had. Then, to swim the river too! Yet there was no other explanation for my reappearance in Pine Hill that morning: they were all satisfied about that. Could it be that I'd started from the second tunnel? And perhaps earlier—in the afternoon? I shook my head. But was I quite sure?

It was nearly midday when I sat down to breakfast. The girl came in, and took a chair opposite me; she poured herself a cup of coffee. "I think it must have been the second tunnel," she remarked, speaking slowly, with eyes of sly amusement over the rim of the cup.

I smiled; but didn't answer her.

She said she would borrow the publican's car, if I liked, and drive me out to get my own car.

"Thank you." I gazed at her as I was eating. I asked, "Is the light in the valley all that you have seen?"

"No."

I waited.

And she said, "This afternoon—do you think you'd be able to get up to the mine again?"

HAVEN'T WE MET BEFORE?
Hesba F. Brinsmead

When the two cars crashed at the intersection, Elly felt nothing at all.

Not even surprise. Her body was numb; frozen; turned to stone; her mind, clear as a bell. Her mind stood back from the scene, an interested onlooker.

The Holden had shot out from the left, just as she came forward from behind the milk tanker, thinking to cross quickly before the lights changed. They'd not seen each other because of the tanker. They'd ground into each other in the middle of the crossways, on the hill slope near Paddington. She knew that her car—well, Denis' car, her brother's car, was a heap of crushed metal. He'd worked through long vacations to earn the down payment on it. This had been the first time he'd let her drive it through the city alone. And the last, now. She'd been hurrying to get home from Peg's house before the storm broke. So had half a million other drivers—deserting beaches, this sultry afternoon, abandoning the racetrack and the ballgame—everyone clogging the streets under the black thunderheads, the rolling purple cloudstacks.

As to the Holden . . . she could only hear things. Voices sounded very clear. "They'll need to lift it" . . . "wait for a blow-torch" . . . "ring the ambulance station."

"Don't move her. Her neck could be broken."

"We'll have to move her!"

"We'd better wait for the police, anyway."

"She'll have to be moved. Get a trestle from that house."

Elly wondered whose neck could be broken. Then it came to her that they were speaking of herself.

A trestle. Yes, she remembered seeing trestles and painters' ladders against the old terrace house near the corner. Being restored, she supposed. There was the usual clutter around it: paint tins, scaffolding, broken plaster. She'd even had time to think that it was unusual for men to be house-painting on a Saturday afternoon, when the rest of the city was taking its fun. Or had been, until the storm threatened. Now the world and his dog were driving pell-mell for their homes, the traffic worse than any weekday crush. She wondered, was it two of the painters who were arguing over her now, where she had been thrown from the car wreckage? The voices were clear again.

"No ambulances! The drivers are out on strike!"

Elly tried to speak to these people, who were doing their best for her. But no sound came. She did not even know if her lips moved, in obedience to her will.

"Here comes the rain! Bucketing down!"

She knew the storm had broken. She could see the sky above her, its blackness riven by rents of red lightning. It was like seeing things happen on a film.

"We'll have to get her into the house."

"You're not supposed to move—"

"We can't let her die in the pouring rain!"

"I think she's already dead, mate. The rain won't trouble her no more."

"We're not sure. We can't leave her here."

"Okay, okay, you win. It don't seem nice, to leave her hair all—"

"Here, shut up and take the other end."

They put her down in a room. There was a smell of new pinewood. The floor where they laid her plank stretcher was deep with curling wood shavings. The scents and sounds were clear—clear and vivid. And—familiar? There was something familiar . . .

"A doctor at the weekend, that's a joke. I'll ring the hospital again."

"How are they going with that blow-torch? Have they freed the other driver?"

"Don't know. What, no lights?"

"No, the electricity's turned off while they do the fittings."

"Might be just as well, in this storm. Electricity! She's everywhere!"

"I'll see if they need a hand with that young feller."

"I'll try the hospital again."

There was a door closing, footsteps retreating . . .

It was a comfort to be in the room, while the storm raged. Elly, with her strangely sharpened hearing, was very much aware of the storm. She liked it. Feeling nothing, yet she was aware of some strange element, linking her with the storm. Thunder growled menacing as mastiffs outside; it shook the old house like a terrier with a rat. Yet the room kept the monsters at bay. They could not claw their way in through the curved bay window. Huge and hungry as they were, the lace curtains defeated them.

"Lace curtains?" mused Elly. "If they're painting and installing light fittings, why lace curtains?"

The rain on the roof was like a million tiny hammers. Elly felt safe from them. Something she had read came back to her. That walls absorb thoughtwaves. And emotions. Everything is made up of waves . . . and electricity. The thoughtwaves in old walls will echo back . . . but between the lace curtains, what a fine aspidistra!

"And that," thought Elly, "is a gas light. They said no light . . . but of course, that is a gas light."

41

It was impossible to say at what point the room became complete. Surely the lace curtains came first ... then the aspidistra, in a—"a *jardinière*," she thought, "a fine *jardinière*!" She did not know when the smell of paint and shavings turned to beeswax and lavender. But the lavender, dried lavender, was in a vase on the mantlepiece. There were two vases, one each end, white china with a black silhouette of a lady in a crinoline dancing with a gentleman in a peruke. Next to the vases were brass candlesticks, and in the exact centre, an ormolu clock. There were brass candlesticks on the piano, too, either side of the filagree walnut panel, backed with pleated silk. There was a rag rug by the brass fender; the sofa and bandy-legged chairs were graced with anti-macassars. Each chair, each picture, was placed just so. She could not understand what position she herself occupied, amid such orderliness. Where, among this decorum, was a body on a painter's trestle?

There was an extraordinary, quite blinding flash of lightning. White light, it was, brilliantly white, playing like a searchlight over walls and furniture, steady, long, seeming endlessly long, so bright that she shut her eyes against its merciless white glare, and even then ... even then ... it was white agony, the intensity of it, through closed eyelids. She felt herself sigh and gasp, through a long and utter silence, while the white light tore at her eyes. Silence—dead silence. Then, at first only a shudder, only a shaking through the fabric of the room, the old house, through the earth under the house, then growing into an all-embracing, rolling roar, came the thunder, roll upon roll, deep, deafening, terrible, worse than the white lightning. Elly thought she screamed, but in that enormous holocaust of sound ...

She was in his arms, struggling, fighting for breath as he crushed the air from her lungs, white light dancing across her eyeballs, her ears ringing with noise, her screams stifled.

Only when she was half-fainting did he loosen his grip, so that she hung like a broken bird in his grasp.

"I won't let you go," Robert was grinding through clenched teeth. "I won't let you go. Oh, Gabrielle, I've hurt you—you're not really hurt, are you? I'd never hurt you, I'd not do that, I love you so much. Say you're not hurt? You can't leave me, you can't go!"

"You . . . you . . . " Still there was no breath in her lungs for speech. She shook. How cold she was. How . . . frightened . . . Now he held her so tender and gently, stroking her wet hair, her cheek, kissing her eyes.

"Oh, Elly, I don't mean to hurt you, it's only when you say you'll leave me. I don't know what I'm doing, such strange feelings come over me. It's because I can't bear it, I can't live without you, you know I can't. If you'll just tell me you didn't mean what you said, just tell me you'll never go away, just tell me."

At last, very faint and shaking, she could form a word or two with her lips.

"All—all right . . . Robert."

"You mean it? You truly mean it?"

Not trusting herself to say more, she nodded her head once. He rocked her now, soothing her. She opened her eyes and looked slantingly up at him, and at the arms holding her.

Yes, he was handsome. No young man could be more so. The black hair that curled on the high, white forehead; the long-lashed dark eyes, set at a strange angle in his aquiline face, predatory and beautiful. His beginnings of a Van Dyke beard! The arms were clad in brown velvet. She remembered how her father would splutter with rage at the very mention of Robert's clothes. "That cockscomb! That—swaggering—mountebank! The clothes of a pirate! A highwayman! What decent, sober Christian would be seen dead or alive in such finery!"

43

It had been his clothes that had first caught her eye and fascinated her. Then it was the mesmerism of the young man himself. His tender voice when he sang, the sweetness of his touch upon the harpsichord which he played in the newly-opened theatre of Sydney Town. It was not until later that she'd discovered his terrifying rages: surely the seeds of madness were in him. Not until later that she'd learned to fear him. Yet, even now, it was love and hate, hate and love. Now—so gentle, so like a child—how could she not love him? How could she want to go? And still she knew that in a moment, the rage could take him, and he'd be a devil.

It was at such a moment that she'd run from this very room—when—how long ago? He'd been like to kill her. Why? Over something so small, they'd already both forgotten! Of course her father had commanded her never to see him more. But it was only when he'd raged, and made her frightened, that she'd run from the room and taken a passing hansom cab. She'd meant to go to her aunt's house; he'd not know the way there. But he'd rushed after her in his dashing, high-wheeled gig. He'd whipped his horse into terror and driven straight into the hansom cab. The driver was injured badly, she was sure. Someone had just shot one of the horses; the other was dead already. He'd brought her back to this room. It was a fine house, which he rented with the money he earned on the theatre stage, for all the town flocked to hear him sing and play. And to perform his strange "mesmerism" act. There were always young girls in the audience, young gentlewomen like herself, reared in sheltered style, who were willing to step up and be mesmerized. But she, only she, had won his heart. Only she had ever come to his parlour. She shuddered. How proud she'd been, that he loved her! And now—how afraid. How afraid . . .

He was whispering, close to her ear. His voice, coloured with Celtic lights and depths, irresistible, was whispering.

44

There was a faint accent on his speech; nobody could guess its origin; he'd told nobody of his homeland or where he'd come from. Among the motley of the Town were Frenchman, Spaniard, swarthy Gipsy. His homeland could be anywhere. "He could come," Elly's father had cried, "from Hades itself, for all we know!" Yet how moving his voice could be. Just to listen, when she was so tired. Just to listen. What was he saying now?

"If ever you leave me, Gabrielle, I'll find you, be it beyond the sea, or over the mountains where none have gone, and I'll bring you back to this room. Time and distance will mean nought to me, my beauty, my dove. You can die, you can hide from me in death, you can take your life away, but I'll bring you back, if it takes a hundred years—to this very room."

He let her go, and stepped in his lightfooted way to the open piano. With one finger he picked out a phrase of music. Thin and clear it sounded, brittle as ice, small as a breath, clear as a flame. It was a phrase of Grieg, of *Solveig's Song*.

On that small delicate note, the last of the thunder died away. There were approaching feet, the sound of heavy workmen's boots. A door opening.

"Here they are, doctor. Maybe past your help."

"We'll see. Make way for that oxygen. Pass my bag."

Summer was over when they wheeled Elly on to the balcony.

But there was still warmth in the sun that streamed over her couch. At the edge of the balcony were the tops of trees, and finches played in them.

"Here's company for you," said the nurse, putting her next to a wheelchair. A guitar leaned against it. A young fellow lay rugged against the breeze, his head tilted back, his eyes closed. Elly studied his face. The black hair curling from a high forehead; beautiful, aquiline features; the beginnings of a Van Dyke beard. It was the face she had seen in her mind, waking and sleeping, these months past. That mouth—cruel, yet sweet. Ruthless. A face that would never give in.

The eyes opened. Dark, strangely slanted.

"Robert?"

There was nothing in the eyes but approval, slight surprise, perhaps embarrassment.

"You—know my name? I suppose they told you."

"You know mine?"

"Oh, yes!" He made a petulant gesture. "Of course. All the nurses have been making sure that I know all about my victim! I mean—anyway, they keep telling me you had the right of way! What a way to meet! At least, may I say that it couldn't have happened to a nicer person?"

He was unashamed, preposterous; and it was impossible not to smile at him.

"I *shouldn't*!" she thought. "I should ask the nurse to wheel me to some other place!" But . . . his smile was as disarming as a child's.

"I don't know what got into me that day." He was like a child, confiding. "I've never had a prang! Never!"

"Are you—all right?"

"Might have a bit of a limp. They tell me your hair will hide the scar. You're still pretty enough to freak out any room full of other girls—if I may say so."

"You're welcome." She closed her eyes. It was like walking down a hill, that would get steeper and steeper, until one would be running too fast to stop. Don't go, don't go on! Yet—where else was there to go?

"Elly—I can call you Elly, can't I?—I know this is an old expression. Corny. A cliché. But—haven't we met before?"

"*Where?*"

He sat frowning; creasing his forehead, trying to place

something, trying to remember. At last he shook his head, exasperated.

"Can't think of the time!"

"Then—we can't have, can we?"

"Suppose not, but—it's a funny thing."

His hand went to the guitar at his side. Without looking at it, he picked out a phrase of melody: the opening notes of *Solveig's Song.*

THE GHOST OF GARTENSCHMUCK
Colin Thiele

The ghost of *Gartenschmuck* was more than a legend. It was a real thing. For thirty years it had been appearing near the main road from Kapunda to Bethel, not far from the grim old house in the Valley.

Some people said there were actually two ghosts—one a tender, womanly spirit like a column of white light, and the other a monstrous ghoul that had almost killed poor Ahmed Singh, the hawker, when he had accidentally camped in *Gartenschmuck* one night long ago before he'd heard that it was haunted. The tender one was the ghost of Maria Rollenberg, a lovely bride who had been murdered on her wedding night thirty years before by her husband, Kreutzer, who himself had then come to a bad end. *Gartenschmuck* was the house they were going to live in after the wedding. It remained empty ever afterwards—a huge sombre place with endless sheds and barns and sties surrounding it like an old fortress or medieval keep. Nobody ever went near it except the Richter boys, who owned the farm now. But even they made sure they were gone before the sun set.

Benny Geister lived with his Uncle Gus a few kilometres away near the foothills, and his best friend, Ossie Schmidt, came from the farm next door. Benny was twelve and Ossie was thirteen, but nobody knew how old Uncle Gus was. They had all seen the ghost of Maria Rollenberg; in fact

Uncle Gus had seen it so often that he had lost count. Twice his horse had bolted when the ghost had confronted them on their way home from the Morning Star Hotel in the midnight moonlight, and once he had actually run over it in his old Ford. But none of them had ever seen the ghost of Kreutzer. Ossie said this was because it never came out into the open, but kept skulking about in the shadows of *Gartenschmuck*.

"He's a nasty piece of work, Kreutzer is," Ossie said with authority one day. "Very nasty and silent."

"How do you know?" Benny asked.

"Because he got Ahmed Singh by the throat and jumped on his chest," Ossie answered, "till he couldn't hardly breathe. He had to run for his life."

"Cor!" said Benny.

"Some ghosts are a noisy lot, screaming and hollering and rattling chains about. But not him."

Benny looked about fearfully. "If a ghost screamed at me, I'd take off."

"It's mainly the English ones that do that," Ossie said reassuringly. "Australian ghosts are mainly pretty quiet."

Benny fidgeted. "This one might be a German ghost. All the people around here came out from Germany. Kreutzer did."

"That's what I'm saying," Ossie answered. "German ghosts are a quiet lot too. Except for the poltergeists."

"Poltergeists?"

"Yes, poltergeists. They're the ones that throw things about."

"Cor, I don't think I like them either," Benny said.

"They knock stuff off the shelves and that. Pick things up and take a shot at you behind your back."

"Jeepers!"

"And they can see in the dark."

"I hate poltergeists," Benny said firmly. "They're the worst of the lot, I reckon."

"You can't see 'em, that's the trouble," Ossie said. "Some people reckon they're black, like the darkness, and that's why."

"Poltergeists are the worst," Benny said earnestly.

"Most ghosts are white." Ossie spoke with clear conviction.

"Are they?"

"Most decent ghosts."

"They're not so bad, white ghosts."

"They still scare the daylights out of you," Ossie said, "but at least you can see what you're up against."

"They'd still scare me," Benny said, nodding his head wholeheartedly. "I wouldn't like any colour of ghost, not after Maria Rollenberg. She frightened the tripe out of me."

A few weeks later Benny's cousin, Arthur, came up from Adelaide to stay on Uncle Gus' farm for a week. Benny disliked him. He had big feet, big ears and an even bigger mouth. He knew everything and he laughed and jeered at the idea of ghosts. Benny felt hemmed in by him, tongue-tied and depressed.

They were out in the stables on the second day, the two of them, and Arthur was rolling all over the place with laughter because Benny had mentioned that Uncle Gus had heard ghostly footsteps on the Bethel road.

Benny detested Arthur more and more. How could he even begin to talk to him? A know-all who didn't know anything, who couldn't even imagine what it was like to be out alone on the ranges in the darkness before dawn, to feel the touch of starlight on his hands, the dark breeze on his cheeks, the witching interplay of moonlight and shadow under the tall trees by the road, the deformed yacca rearing up suddenly at his side in the gloom like an inquisitive

50

gooseneck, the touch of a rabbit's fur in the cold of a winter's morning, the magic of a still dam shining in the darkness like a patch of night sky surprised in a valley, the sound that was almost the sound of breathing on the loneliness of the hills, the unheard footsteps on the Bethel road, the unseen speed of poltergeists ... How could he, Benny, ever talk to someone like Arthur?

"And as for Uncle Gus and the ghostly footsteps on the road," Arthur was saying, "really you have to be joking. How many drunks hear pink elephants stomping around every night of the week!"

Benny was getting too angry and too tired to argue any more, but he felt that he should throw out at least one last challenge.

"What about the ghost of Maria Rollenberg?" he asked fiercely. "Dozens of people have seen her, and so have I."

Arthur laughed and slapped him on the shoulder. "Do you believe everything you see, Ben? What about the bloke who saws a lady in half at the show—all without blood?" He paused because he reckoned he had Benny reeling. "Optical illusion, Ben! You think you see something, but it's really something quite different. Like flying saucers."

"That wasn't a flying saucer," Benny said stubbornly. "It was a galloping ghost."

Arthur rolled about in agonies of delight at that. "Galloping ghosts is about right, Ben. A patch of moonlight cantering along between two clouds, or car headlights reflected from something a long way away, like a window or a mirror; that's how you make ghosts in the night."

Benny was inwardly exhausted. He was in such a state of rage and frustration and conflict that he felt he either had to punch Arthur very hard in the stomach or burst into tears and fling himself down with his face pressed into the old saddle rugs by the door of the stable where they were standing.

51

Luckily Ossie came up just at that moment. Benny was so relieved that he almost flung himself on his shoulder instead, which would have shocked Ossie to the bone.

"Benny! Hey, Benny!" Ossie was leaning forward with the haste of his walking—a sure sign of important news. He was about to pour it all out to Benny when he spied Arthur standing in the doorway. He stopped short, recognizing him from previous visits.

"Good day."

"Good afternoon, Oscar."

"Up for a holiday?"

"Yes, for one week of the vacation."

"Having a good time?"

"I've only just arrived. I've been talking to Ben, telling him how ridiculous all these ghost stories are."

"Pretty stupid are they, d'you reckon?"

"Ludicrous."

They were all silent for a while. It would have been a difficult time if Arthur hadn't been called inside just then, leaving Ossie and Benny alone.

"What a creep!" Benny said,

"He's a real squirt, ain't he?" Ossie agreed. But then he remembered his news and forgot all about Arthur in the excitement of it. "Hey, Benny," he said, lowering his voice conspiratorially in case the shed's ears were listening, "d'you know what old Kronkie's got on the notice in his window?" Kronkie was Mr Eddie Kronk, butcher, of Kapunda, who paid Benny twenty cents a pair for his rabbit carcasses and put up all kinds of clever slogans such as "Pleasant Meating", and "From Meat to You", to attract more customers.

Benny looked at Ossie excitedly. He could tell from his friend's face that he was the bearer of big news. "No. What?"

Ossie gloated. "He wants pigeons. As many as he can get."

"Pigeons?"

"Pigeons. That's what it says on the notice."

Benny was deflated. "What's he want pigeons for?"

Ossie sensed Benny's disappointment and was ready with the facts. "I asked him that."

"What did he say?"

"Squobbin aspic."

Benny wrinkled up his face in disgust. "Squobbin aspic? What's that supposed to mean?"

Ossie was just as mystified as Benny was. "I don't know. Maybe it's the name of the bloke down in Adelaide that he's going to sell 'em to."

"Sounds a snotty sort of name. Are you sure it wasn't squabblin'?"

"Could've been." Ossie dismissed the finer points of the words as irrelevant. "Anyway, it doesn't matter. The important thing is that he's willing to pay fifty cents a pair."

Benny nearly fell over the hitching rail near the stable door. "Fifty cents! Holy crackers!"

Ossie was grinning far back around the sides of his head like a happy hippopotamus. "That's right. I checked twice, to make sure."

"Why's he paying so much?" Benny asked suspiciously. "The old goanna only pays me twenty cents for rabbits."

Ossie shrugged. "It's for the Gourmets, he said."

"Gourmets? Who the heck are they?"

"Don't know. But that's what old Kronkie said."

Benny puzzled with the name and tasted it on his tongue. "Must be a religious crowd—like the Catholics. Maybe they only eat pigeons on Fridays, or something. They must be pretty keen if they're willing to pay that much for pigeons."

Ossic's eyes gleamed above his cheeks like a chubby pig's and his big leathery ears stood out stiff with delight. "That's why I came straight over," he said. "That price might only last for a week."

Benny eased himself up on to the hitching rail and turned his attention to matters of practical finance. "How many d'you reckon we can get at your place? Twenty?"

"About that."

"There wouldn't be more than ten or a dozen around here," Benny said. "Too many blooming cats."

"A dozen's a dozen," Ossie said profoundly.

Benny was not wildly enthusiastic. "So we'd get maybe thirty altogether. That's fifteen pairs. Seven or eight dollars." He considered the point for a second. "I s'pose it's easier than trapping rabbits."

"I'll say it is," Ossie said. "Just go along the rafters with a torch as soon as it gets dark and lift 'em straight off into a bag. Like picking peaches."

"It is easier than rabbits," Benny admitted.

"'Course it is," said Ossie. "Only takes a few seconds. Four or five a minute, easy. Twenty-five cents a time."

Benny's eyes were beginning to shine too. "A dollar a minute," he said. "I wish there were more pigeons."

Ossie looked about furtively to make sure that nobody was watching or listening. "I know where we can get more," he said softly. "Hundreds and hundreds more."

Benny sensed some:.`g suspicious and clandestine in Ossie's manner and edged back a little. "You're not going to pinch 'em, Ossie?"

Ossie kept on smiling idiotically and shook his head vigorously. "No. Everything's above board. I've even got proper permission to take 'em."

Benny was nonplussed. "Hundreds of 'em?" he repeated.

"Hundreds," replied Ossie.

"I give up. Where?"

Ossie's eyes were suddenly dark and piercing; he was breathing in a suppressed kind of way.

"*Gartenschmuck!*"

Benny shot up off the hitching rail as if he'd been stuck by the upthrust point of a bag needle. "*Gartenschmuck?*"

Ossie was eager and wide-eyed. "What d'you say?"

Benny was aghast. "You must be off your crumpet. *Gartenschmuck!* In the *night!*"

"It would only be early dark. Straight after sundown."

"No thanks! Not any sort of dark. Not in that place."

"I'll bet it's not half as bad as everyone says."

"Half of Maria Rollenberg is more than I can take," said Benny. "Even a quarter of a ghost would put the wind up me."

Ossie tried a different line. "The Richter boys are always working around the place—in the stables and sheep-yards and that. They never see anything."

"Yes," Benny answered. "In the *day*-time!"

"Well, the early evening is nearly the day-time."

"Except that it's dark," Benny said ironically; "it's a sort of dark day-time."

Ossie persevered. "I watched it all day, nearly, through Dad's telescope, and it was just as calm as your place is."

"That's not too calm with Uncle Gus around."

"The Richter boys were crutching and drafting. They had their horses there, and the dogs were running around as happy as Larry. That's when I went over and asked about the pigeons."

"What did they say?"

"Glad to get rid of 'em. Ought to pay us a bounty, Herbie said, just to clean 'em out. Like a plague they are, scratching out the seed, mucking up the water troughs, playing up hell's delight."

Benny was far from converted. "What did they say about ... about the place being haunted?"

"Nothing. Just asked if we were game, that's all."

"There you are," said Benny. "They were having you on."

"No they weren't. They want us to take the pigeons. Honest."

"Why don't *they* take 'em. You never see them there after dark."

"No reason to. They got more money than they know what to do with."

The mention of money brought avarice back into Ossie's eyes. He stepped forward and took Benny eagerly by the sleeve. "Listen, Ben, you should've seen the pigeons that were there, even in the day-time. The place was crawling with them. They've been nesting and breeding there for donkey's years and nobody's ever disturbed them. They're all over the stables and everywhere—on the rafters, in the straw thatch of the old sheds, on top of the posts, in the forks of the uprights, even in the house."

"I'm not going in there," Benny said quickly, backing away from Ossie. "Not in the old house."

"We won't have to," Ossie answered persuasively. "There's a fortune in the sheds."

Benny laughed wryly. "You're always on about fortunes, Os."

"It *is* a fortune, Benny—for blokes like you and me. I reckon we could get four hundred pigeons from over there in a couple of nights. Two hundred each. And that's a hundred dollars."

"A hundred dollars!"

"Work it out for yourself." Ossie paused and looked at Benny cunningly. "You could have your motor-bike even before you could get a licence, nearly."

It was clear that Benny was wavering. "You reckon there are that many? Honest?"

Ossie swept his arms around like a tycoon gloating over his estate. "It's just a start. We could get a thousand pairs if we wanted to. Five hundred dollars."

That was too much for Benny. "Jeepers. Five hundred dollars!"

"We'll never get another chance like it, I'll tell you that."

Benny seemed to take a deep breath. "All right, I'll come."

"Cock of the heap, old rooster!" said Ossie exultingly. "I knew you would."

"When?" said Benny uncertainly. "Not . . . not tonight?"

"No, we'll do ours and yours tonight. Just to get our hands in. Then tomorrow night we'll have a crack at the big money." He was so excited by his own enthusiasm that he ran around in a circle plucking imaginary pigeons down from the rails and posts. *"Gartenschmuck,"* he chanted, making a kissing noise with his lips, "we love you, *Gartenschmuck; Schmuck! Schmuck! Schmuck!"*

While he was watching Ossie's money-dance Benny had a sudden thought. "Hey," he said, "what about Arthur?"

Ossie stopped short for a split second and then went on dancing and catching airy pigeons. "We'll take him with us," he said.

"What? That toad?"

"He'll be useful. Fetch and carry. Hold things. Lug the stepladder around and tie up the bags." Ossie paused. "And if we meet a nasty we'll push him out in front." He tittered gleefully. "Maybe a poltergeist'll twist his ears off."

But Benny was never one to invite the anger of the spirits. "You can talk," he said soberly. "If a poltergeist gets hold of your ears, Ossie, you'll be done for."

All the arrangements went smoothly. To Benny's surprise nobody objected to his idea of adding a little pigeon-catching to his rabbit-trapping enterprises. Uncle Gus even applauded it. "Very goot," he said warmly. "Pigeons do not'ing but *Dreck-Dreck-Dreck* all over d' place. On d' saddles, on d' rugs, on your head even. Best to screw dere necks."

Of course Benny didn't say anything about *Gartenschmuck.* They didn't tell Arthur either, because they knew he would go clacking all over the place with the news. They just said they were going pigeon-catching for the next two or three nights to help butcher Kronk with supplies for the Gourmets. The first night went brilliantly. The pigeons seemed to sit mesmerized on the rafters in the beam of the torch, and all the boys had to do was pick them off and pop them into the big bags that Arthur held ready. It was just as Ossie had predicted. When they'd cleaned out Uncle Gus's sheds they went over to Ossie's place and did the same thing there. It was incredible. In less than two hours they had more than forty—almost without effort.

"Ten dollars," Ossie said, gloating. "It's money for jam."

"Is it ever," said Benny. "Ding-a-ling-a-ling!"

Ossie's eyes were shining. "Wait till tomorrow night. We'll be millionaires."

Even Arthur seemed mildly interested—not because of the money, which he said was peanuts, but because of the adventure of it all. Skulking about in old sheds at night, pin-pointing the quarry, seizing it quietly and firmly without any fuss, and then popping it into a big bag like a safe-breaker's loot—it was a new and unusual experience. He was buoyed up, too, by Ossie's praise.

"Good on you, Arthur," Ossie said loudly and exuberantly when the bag closed over another victim. "You're worth your weight in pigeon droppings!"

"Where are we going tomorrow night?" Arthur asked.

"We'll find some more spots," Ossie answered vaguely. "I'll call for you and Benny just after sundown."

And so the *Gartenschmuck* adventure began. They set out in the twilight, walking quickly down the Nagala Creek and then skirting the outriders of the range until they came to the knoll that looked down on the old homestead. Arthur held the bags and Ossie and Benny carried the light stepladder between them. The gloom had deepened, but there was just enough light still left in the sky to throw up the silhouettes of the ridges and the outlines of the farm buildings that were clustered in the valley below the house. Their size astounded Benny—stables, sheds, barns, tanks, sties, and mustering yards—all grouped around a central keep that looked like the sheltered market-place of an ancient village; and beyond it stood the house, a dark monstrous shape in the darkness.

"Cor," said Benny in an unnecessary whisper, "big, ain't it?"

"Huge," Ossie answered in a subdued voice. "No wonder it gives people the creeps."

Benny's enthusiasm for pigeon-hunting was ebbing fairly quickly. "D'you think . . . d'you think we'll be able to find our way?" he asked.

Even Arthur was hushed and tense. "D'you mean nobody lives there at all?" he asked.

"Only ghosts," said Ossie without thinking, and then wished he hadn't said it because it set all three of them on edge.

Arthur was the first to put on some front again. "There are no such things so the place must be empty."

"Sure," said Ossie. "Except for pigeons. Millions of 'em. We'll make a fortune tonight, I tell you."

Arthur was clutching the empty bags. "How are we going to carry them all back?"

"What we can't carry we'll leave and pick up tomorrow." Ossie moved forward. "Come on, down this track. Better lift your big feet."

They filed down silently to the valley floor and moved forward through the darkness to the first group of stables. Ossie was a born leader and he had spied out the land carefully beforehand. "This way," he whispered cautiously. "They ought to be thick in here." It was a huge horse-stable, sixty or seventy metres long, fitted with dozens of stalls and a feed trough like a wooden canal that ran from one end to the other. Ossie flashed the torch briefly along the rafters and cross-struts. There were pigeons everywhere, bunched up in long lines like starlings on a fence.

"Look at 'em," Ossie whispered fiercely and greedily. "Like beads on a string."

He switched off the torch and for a second or two they couldn't see a thing until their eyes adjusted to the darkness again. Arthur blundered into the stepladder and reeled back against Ossie.

"Watch it! Watch it!" Ossie hissed. "We don't want to let every flaming thing know that we're here."

"What thing?" Benny asked nervously.

Ossie ignored him. "Come on, this way. We'll start from one end and work down." He was jubilant at the certainty of the catch. "It'll be like taking cobs off the corn."

"You mean corn off the cob," said Arthur.

"All right, Einstein," Ossie answered tartly. "I mean peas in a pot."

"That's dirty," said Benny. "You mean peas in a pod."

"That's what I said! Now stop clowning, you two, and get this ladder up there."

They pushed and manoeuvred for a moment. "That's it. Now, Arthur, ready with the bag. Benny, you steady the steps." And Ossie climbed up lightly for the first assault on their unsuspecting prey.

For half an hour they worked stealthily and efficiently, taking it in turns to stand at the top of the stepladder seizing the pigeons. By now their routine was well established. The light-beam flashed on to the roosting bird, two hands closed over its body firmly and evenly to prevent any struggling or the noisy flapping of wings, the neck of the bag opened momentarily to admit the new victim and then closed tightly again after it.

"Good work," whispered Ossie as they made the fiftieth capture. "Benny, you're deadly with that torch. Laser Ben, they call him."

They moved the ladder stealthily as they worked their way down the stable. "Better not put too many in one bag," Benny said. "It's cruel, and they might die."

"I've used three already," Arthur answered. "We're going to run out of bags."

"Then we'll lock up the ones we can't take and come back for them in the morning."

"Where are you going to lock 'em up?" asked Benny. "In the dunny?"

"We'll find a room or a bit of a barn somewhere. We're not stopping this bonanza just because we haven't got anything to put them in."

When they had cleaned out the stable as well as they could they moved on to the old cowshed and dairy next door. Here they were less successful. The building was far more decrepit, with tumbledown walls and debris all over the floor, and the pigeons seemed wilier and more restless. Twice Arthur missed one altogether and it went flying off frantically into the night; once Ossie himself let one wrench its wings free and it filled the night with feathers and flapping; and once Benny would have capsized the ladder altogether if Ossie hadn't lunged forward to brace it at the last minute.

"Careful! Careful!" he hissed urgently. "Hell's teeth, do you want to crack open your melon?"

Benny came down, crestfallen. "I reckon it's time we packed up, Os."

Ossie looked up, as if to consult the sun. "What's the time?"

"I don't know," Arthur answered. "We've been here a good while."

"How long?"

"A few hours. Longer, maybe."

"Easy, I reckon," Benny said.

Ossie wiped his forehead to get rid of dust and feathers rather than perspiration. "It's later than I thought, then.

We'd better get back or everyone will be wondering where the heck we are."

"Come on, then." Benny was all for retreating while things were still going well.

"What about the pigeons?" Arthur asked. "We can't possibly carry all these."

"How many have we got?" Benny said.

Ossie shone the torch on the bulging sacks. "Couple of hundred, near enough. Fifty dollars' worth." He swept the beam around lavishly. "And we've hardly touched the surface. We can keep this going for a week." Benny pointed to the sacks. "We can't carry 'em in those things," he said, "not as many as that. They'd die, half of them."

"We'll have to leave some here, and come back for them in the morning," said Ossie. "Better look around for something to put them in."

They were about to move out to search the other sheds when a faint gust of wind moved over them momentarily and the night was suddenly filled with stealthy sounds—not only the secret creaking of timber and the rustling of thatch, but the darkness itself moving like a hushed tide, a mysterious breathing amid the desolate buildings.

Another gust came and went, and this time a low note moaned faintly with it and was gone again—a muted wind wail, perhaps, or a human being mourning privately and desperately in the inner recesses of the old house. It stung the boys like ice.

"What . . . what was that?" Benny asked, cold goose pimples pricking his neck.

"Put out that torch!" Ossie whispered to Arthur. "Listen!"

They waited motionless, holding their breaths. But there was nothing more.

"Only the wind," murmured Ossie at last.

"I . . . I think we ought to go," Benny whispered.

"What, and leave all the pigeons in the bags?"

"I reckon there's . . . something, something else besides us around here." Benny's forebodings were enough to set all three of them trembling again, including Arthur who seemed to have dropped his former bravado like a pair of wet pants.

"Enough of that talk, Benny," Ossie hissed. "You give a bloke the creeps."

They were huddling together in the darkness, touching one another for the comfort of human contact. Suddenly they caught their breaths again and a little thrill of terror swept each one; for a low moan rose and fell once more, and faded into a sigh, into a kind of rustle like the movement of huge mothwings in the gloom. Benny's hair stood up as stiff as sticks.

"It's . . . it's M . . . M . . . Maria R . . . Rollenberg," he said in a hushed whisper. "I told you we should have made a run for it."

"How . . . how d'you know it's her?"

"That's the way she sounds. Uncle Gus has heard it lots of times."

Ossie turned to Arthur. "Give us the torch, Arthur," he whispered. "You're shaking so much you're rattling the batteries."

"She's t . . . tall and white," Benny went on, "d . . . dressed like a bride."

They waited tensely. "To meet her would be bad enough, but Kreutzer'd be worse."

"Who's K . . . Kreutzer?" asked Arthur in a strangled sort of croak.

"The bridegroom. They reckon he murdered her and then killed himself. They were never seen again."

"L . . . let's go, Oscar," Arthur pleaded in a wheedling tone.

"I . . . I'm going, Os," whispered Benny. "You coming or not?"

"All right," Ossie whispered back, rather relieved that the

decision had been taken out of his hands, "but don't blame me if we lose half the pigeons."

"Which way?" asked Arthur.

"Round here; careful!"

They were up near the far end of the dairy. To reach the track down the valley they either had to retrace their steps through the cowshed and horse-stables, or take a short cut across the central courtyard surrounded by the other buildings. Ossie decided on the short cut.

They moved out cautiously into the open air, holding on to one another. It was very dark now. A milky moonstain was travelling fast behind the banks of clouds, but it was so erratic and so hidden that it gave no light. If anything, it emphasized the darkness instead. "Mind your feet," Ossie whispered. "And keep close together." There was no need to give the warning because Benny and Arthur were treading on his heels, fearful that at any minute they would feel a clammy grip and find themselves walking hand in hand with something from beyond the grave. Ossie groped his way along the outside wall of the dairy towards the courtyard, leaving the drafting yards, sties, breeding pens, and old smokehouse on his left. The wall was high—six or seven metres at least—because it formed part of the loft and barn beyond. Even in the thick darkness Ossie felt dwarfed by it. Then he reached the gap where a gate had once led into the yard, passed through it, and turned sharply left. Benny and Arthur followed.

And there it was! Rearing up in the air before them. More horrible than anything in life or death—evil and silent and ghostly. And so close to them that they could have touched it. It was huge. Three metres high at least, floating a metre above the ground, towering above them with its arms stretched upwards and outwards as if crucified to the night, its head faceless; its torso white and wraith-like. Yet unmistakably a body, a form. A supernatural being.

After the first blood-chilling shock, the gurgling *Ar-r-r-k* from Ossie and the thump of the torch falling from his hands, they stood frozen for a part-second, their hearts seemingly no longer beating, their blood frigid, their eyes starting from their sockets. The monstrous apparition sensed their presence and turned towards them.

And then they fled. Screaming. Back through the open gateway, back past the wall of the dairy, the tumbledown cowshed, falling and stumbling, colliding into one another, crying out for help, catching up and being left behind, stampeding, never looking back, feeling the monstrous pursuit, the evil presence breathing close, the chill clutch at their shoulders, running on and on, straining away from the sheds and buildings, the diabolic house, the cursed boundaries of *Gartenschmuck*. Fleeing, fleeing, fleeing.

By a miracle they kept together in the end, guided by their panting cries and their wheezing, and the shapes of their silhouettes as they reached the top of the knoll at the head of the valley. And there, for the first time, they looked back, and paused and finally sank down on the grass exhausted, speechless, shattered, with bloodied knees and heaving chests, and minds too shaken even to comprehend.

"Jesus!" said Ossie, sincerely and piously. "Dear Lord God Jesus!"

Arthur was lying on his elbows, sobbing, trying to get his breath back. Benny was crying from shock.

"Oh God!" Ossie repeated, panting desperately, "Oh God!"

They lay there wheezing and retching for a long while.

"Did ... did you get ... get a look at it?" Ossie asked at last.

A shudder seemed to well up from the soles of Benny's boots and swept over him so violently that his whole body shook. "Ur-r-r-r-r-gh! Horrible! Horrible! Horrible!"

"It was ... was a ... a ... ghost!" Arthur said at last.

Ossie shuddered too. "Gr-r-r-rh! And so close I could have touched the stinking thing."

"A real ghost," Arthur repeated, as if still unwilling to believe it.

"And not ... not Maria Rollenberg," wheezed Benny. "So ... it ... it must've been ... Kreutzer. Guarding the place."

Ossie roused himself then and crawled up on to his hands and knees. "We'd better keep going," he said, looking back fearfully towards *Gartenschmuck,* "before it decides to come after us."

Arthur agreed. "Better hurry."

Benny was rummaging about with the inside seams of his trouser legs.

Ossie stood up. "Come on, Benny! What are you hassling about with down there?"

"Well that's the last straw," said Benny. "I've wet my pants."

POINT OF CONTACT
Celia Syred

That Saturday afternoon I was at a loose end. Pam was out with her boyfriend, I was making no headway on the designs I was working on, and the flat (if two rooms and a kitchen contrived on the balcony could be called a flat) was empty to echoing point. My financial situation was so gruesome that I could not possibly afford the fare home, and hitch-hiking was definitely out—I had promised my parents. I was properly in the doldrums when the phone rang. It was my cousin Francesca from Double Bay.

"Can you come over, Vicky? I've a few friends popping in. Stay for the weekend. Bring someone with you if you like. Cheerio! see you." And she rang off before I could tell her I would be on my own.

I was quite pleased. I hadn't seen her for months. Francesca and my widowed aunt had taken over the job of restoring the old family home, which had been tenanted for as long as I could remember by a succession of diplomatic and migratory families of one kind and another. For some reason no member of the family had lived there for a long time. It's the sort of house that is too big for most families nowadays; expensive to maintain and not of sufficient historical importance to warrant the notice of the National Trust. There are still a few houses like that in our harbour-side suburbs, many now drowned in high-rise units, some existing sordidly as flats and rooms for the not-so-affluent.

I remembered Brooksby as a tall house flanked by two wings with a big kitchen at the rear, built on by an embassy which had entertained a great deal. This was before the embassies had folded their tents and stolen away to Canberra. At a little distance from the main building I recalled a carriage-house with stables, then steps down to a disused tennis-court and a jungle of neglected trees and shrubs, where huge hunter spiders lurked and ginger plants luxuriated. At that time the place had not appealed to me, but now, with the wave of nostalgia sweeping over most of us, a new interest in our pile of mouldering stone stirred in me.

Aunt Jessie had planned to refurnish the house, as far as possible, with the original furniture, most of which had been relegated to the attics, where it had been stacked extremely carelessly, necessitating a great deal of careful restoration. But this was right up her street. In fact, my aunt had opened an antique shop in Double Bay and went overseas and interstate regularly to buy up Victoriana and Edwardiana and anything else that took her fancy. The interior of Brooksby was more or less early twentieth century, although the house itself—that is, the original bit in the middle—dated back to about 1830. Cesca's training as an interior decorator dovetailed well into her mother's business and I was dying to talk to her about my favourite period. I was training to be a dress designer and had bouts of enthusiasm—at the moment being completely besotted with the 'twenties. I loved the fluid lines of the designs of the young Chanel, Schiaparelli, and Lucien Lelong; the softness of materials contrasting so boldly with the hard little cloche hats and the hair-styles with precise marcel waves emphasising tiny heads and showing the delicious line of the nape of the neck.

I decided to wear my copy of an early Paul Poiret—a knee-length pleated skirt topped by a jumper with elbow-length sleeves and a bateau neckline. I gave my short, sleek bob a quick comb through, conscious that it suited my small nose, high cheek-bones and long neck. I felt fresh and free without all that long hair that I was so sick of! I was ready for a change. I was bored with skirts up round my thighs; the longer skirts were so soft and feminine, so grown-up. I told myself that as a dress-design student it was my job to be in the forefront of fashion, but frankly I think nostalgia for an age I had never known had me in its sentimental grip. Perhaps I had been born thirty years too late.

Sitting in the bus, I thought back to the night before when some friends had dropped in and the conversation had got round to the supernatural and ghosts. Patrick had said that ghosts were lost souls who couldn't let go of life in this dimension. I'd heard this theory before and wasn't particularly interested until he began to enlarge upon it. His theory was that many ghosts lay dormant or went unnoticed until a set of circumstances relevant to their past lives set the machinery in motion once more.

"We are all more or less mechanical," he said, "computerized if you like—some call it Fate—from the moment of birth. When a record gets stuck in a groove it only needs a coincidence or accumulation of circumstances to get it started again. Given a set of relevant circumstances," he went on, "with the stage set for the tragedy or whatever (it's usually a tragedy of some sort that bungs up the works) there's a point of contact, and we, the ones in this particular point of time" (we'd all groaned at this expression beloved of television speakers) "could find ourselves completely involved in a replay of the happening."

Pam had dug me in the ribs. "Mind you don't get stuck in the 'Gatsby' era with a ghost!"

I laughed, but she was right in a sense; it was almost an obsession with me, this preoccupation with the 'twenties. I loved it all: the clothes, the life-style, the cinemas instead of the goggle-box, everything about it. I would have loved to

69

live then. Probably it would burn itself out eventually, to be replaced by some other enthusiasm, but at the moment I was completely absorbed in it.

The bus dropped me off at the top of Ocean Avenue and I walked down towards the bay. The harbour scintillated and shimmered in the heat as I turned off between the two pillars with *Brooksby* cut in the stone and went up the long drive with its English oaks on one side and tall poplars on the other. I noticed that the old gate was now spruce with paint and the broken hinges mended. I turned the bend in the drive and saw the house, its back almost against the old, convict-built wall, where even in the hottest summer the water trickled down and ferns grew in the cracks. I could well imagine the ghosts of the wretched prisoners haunting the place with echoes of their misery and desperation. The wall was immensely high and the houses above looked down into Brooksby's chimney-pots. In front, the ground dropped sheer to the garden below where a magnificent magnolia grew. It always reminded me of funerals. I shivered and went on past the diamond-paned sitting-room windows in the left wing and up the steps on to the polished wood of the entrance portico, whose roof stretched out over the driveway. I wondered how many carriages had halted in its shade to disgorge opulently-dressed guests for some elaborate function.

Inside the cool, dim entrance hall I paused, remembering what a battering the house had taken from its various tenants and how neglected it had looked when I had last seen it. I was staggered at the changes my aunt and cousin and assorted workmen had made. Most of the original furniture and fittings had been restored and more added in keeping with the decor. I put down my bag and went through the archway into the dining-room, with its long, ornate table, chairs and sideboard (made in Hong Kong for a forbear) all miraculously restored, the dark elaborately-carved wood glowing softly; then on into the breakfast-room and the old kitchen beyond. I came to a halt against the blank wall where the door leading into the embassy-built kitchen should have been. "So they knocked it down. What a good idea," I murmured, "it was an eyesore." I went on through the drying-yard into the laundry just as a figure flitted across the open doorway which led to the butler's pantry.

"Hi, Cesca!" I cried, catching a glimpse of fair hair. But the girl in the butler's pantry wasn't my cousin. She was busy opening cupboard doors—one wall was lined with cupboards—and I saw they were stacked with silver and glass, a fantastic array, the sort of thing wealthy houses used to have at the turn of the century, most of which has now found its way into antique shops. Someone had been hard at work cleaning it, for it sparkled and gleamed, holding my eyes so that I felt almost hypnotized. There was a saucer of plate-powder and a cloth on the terrazo beside the sink. A bit ·old-fashioned I thought, in these days of patent silver-cleaning liquids.

The girl made a little exclamation of satisfaction as she found what she was looking for, a slender silver vase. She filled it at the sink and arranged three beautiful roses in it, then looked at me and smiled. Her hair was fair, that ashen fairness that was once called platinum blonde; like a silver cap on her head, the marcelled waves catching the light. Very trendy, I thought approvingly. Her face was small and rather plump, with the tenuous eyebrows of the 'twenties, rather dark lipstick and long earrings dangling from tiny ears. I burned with envy as I looked covertly at her dress: the fluidity of chiffon splashed with multi-coloured flowers, the handkerchief hem, the narrow gold belt and strings of pearls round the low round neck, were straight out of *The Boy Friend*. Where on earth had she found those shoes with the straps and small curved heels and the flesh-coloured stockings with the sheen of rayon? I had haunted Paddy's Market and found nothing remotely like them.

"Hello," I said, following her out into the passage where she put the vase on the telephone-table. I noticed that the telephone was the real old sort with two pieces to pick up, one for the ear and one for the mouth. I gave Aunt Jessie top marks for attention to detail and wondered if she had found it in the attics with the rest of the furniture. "I suppose Cesca is upstairs changing," I went on, "I'm her cousin, Vicky."

"I'm Violet," she said in a husky little voice, giving the roses a last gentle touch with polished finger-nails. She was really very pretty, I decided, not beautiful or *jolie-laide*, but simply pretty, like a flower.

"I like your dress, Violet. It looks like vintage Patou."

"Thank you," she said, "actually it's a Vionnet. I rather like it too."

"It's super," I enthused. "Now, let's go and find Cesca." I led the way back into the main hall, for I had come full-circle.

Just then we heard the *Vrumb! vrumb!* of a powerful motor and a red sports car complete with straps round its long bonnet roared past the entrance on its way to the carriage-house as Cesca came hurtling down the stairs.

"That must be Michael and some of the crowd in his latest car," she said. "Vicky, I put your bag in the room next to mine." She went on out to the portico and I followed with Violet floating behind, her musky scent giving out little explosions of perfume like some exotic flower. Cesca looked very attractive in a silky Chanel-type cardigan suit from one of Double Bay's most expensive boutiques. Her flaxen hair was fashionably flat on top and curling round her face and neck. Very evocative of the between-the-wars, but not nearly as convincing as Violet. I made up my mind to ask Violet where she had found her Vionnet, which Sydney flea-market or Church bazaar had been hiding such a treasure.

The rather mixed bag of Cesca's guests, some of whom I

knew, streamed into the house, followed by Michael, a young actor on his way up. He had landed a small but interesting part in a weekly television serial set in Sydney between the two world wars. It was a family saga and had been extremely popular right from the start. Michael's almost total identification with his part seemed to flow over into his daily life. With his hair short-back-and-sides for the part, he went round Sydney impeccably dressed in Gatsby-type clothes. My aunt said he reminded her of Jack Buchanan, a matinèe idol of her youth. He made the long-haired youths look scuffy and juvenile. It was certainly a good gimmick, for his face was soon seen everywhere; in television commercials, on hoardings, in magazines. Even his car was a lovingly restored 1928 Morgan sports model. I found him pleasant enough. He had the reputation of being something of a ladykiller, but I always had the impression that he was an ambitious lad who would let nothing stand in the way of his work. I could understand this—I'm a bit that way myself. I would have given my eye-teeth to have had the designing of the 'twenties costumes for *The Sydney Story*.

I could see that he was taken with Violet the minute he set eyes on her; the attraction was mutual and inevitably they drifted off into a quiet corner where they sat talking as if in a special world of their own. They seemed completely cut off from the rest of the party; almost as if they were existing in another time-slot. Strangely enough, no one remarked on it or seemed to notice, even when Cesca put a recording of *That's My Baby* on the turntable and they got up to Charleston expertly on the parquet floor. I knew that Michael must have learned it for his part in *The Sydney Story*, but where had Violet learned to Charleston with such abandon?

I was so intrigued by this incursion into the way of life of my favourite era that I looked out a tango and put that on the turntable, watching their reaction. They were beautiful to watch, both completely absorbed in the dance; Violet's eyes sparkled, her hair falling round her face in corrugated locks and the vintage Vionnet floated and twisted round her boyish little figure. Michael was like a man in a dream, his eyes fixed on his partner. They looked like two people in love. I felt uneasy, as if I were spying on something very private. I didn't particularly want to join the free-style dancers in their gyratings, or the earnest group arguing about ecology, so I went upstairs and out on to the balcony overlooking the harbour. About ten minutes later, I heard feet running down the portico steps below in the direction of the carriage-house. As I listened to the sound of Michael's car starting up, a feeling of impending disaster overwhelmed me. I ran down the back-stairs and on to the drive just in time to see a streak of red with a silver head in the driving seat disappear round the bend in the drive. A second after there was a tremendous roar, so close it seemed to burst in my own head, and then the sound of splintering glass. I ran down to the gates, expecting to see the wreckage of Michael's car and Violet's body.

It was so strange. Everything was going on as if nothing had happened; there was no car, no Violet, only traffic streaming down the hill from the main road, people watering their gardens, walking to and fro from the bay and the shopping-centre. I ran to the corner where the road curved round to join the Old South Head Road, but there was no wrecked car in sight, no horrified spectators, no police-car speeding to the scene; only the water of the bay glittering mockingly. I sat on a bench, feeling rather shaken and very silly. I must have imagined it, my eyes had played me tricks, my ears had been listening to noises inside my own head. It was a humid, heavy day, the air like a hot wet blanket. After some minutes I got up and walked back just as Michael drove out in his car without seeing me. I met the rest of the party leaving to go to a discotheque.

Cesca was plumping up cushions and straightening

chairs. I began to help her. "Cesca," I asked, "Have you seen Violet anywhere?"

"Violet? Do you mean the girl Michael cottoned on to? She must have left with him. Who is she, Vicky?"

"Who is she?" I repeated, "Don't ask me!"

"Didn't you bring her with you?"

"No, I came alone. I thought she was your house-guest; she seemed to know her way around."

Cesca shrugged her shoulders. "A gate-crasher probably. Since Michael is become so well-known he gets his share of fans. Anyway it doesn't really matter."

I took up a tray of dirty glasses. "No, I suppose not."

"We'll wash up in the embassy kitchen, there's more room there," said Cesca.

I put the tray down with shaking hands. "I thought you'd pulled it down."

"We changed our minds. Mother thought the big kitchen and the old servants' annexe would make a beaut flat." She looked keenly at me. "Vicky, you look awful. Sit down and we'll both have a long cool drink. This kind of gloomy, brooding atmosphere gets me down too."

"Yes, it must be the weather," I replied just as my aunt drove her car into the carriage-house and then came into the house by the side-door.

"A cool drink, Mother?"

"Thanks, I could do with it. Well, Vicky, what do you think of the old house now?" My aunt didn't wait for a reply but went on: "We decided to turn the back part into flats and live in the main part ourselves."

I nodded. "Cesca told me."

"Have you seen what we've done to the butler's pantry?" continued my aunt. "It makes a lovely little kitchen and shower. Small but adequate, as the adverts say, stainless-steel sink and all!"

My head seemed to clear suddenly. "Has Brooksby any ghosts, Aunt Jessie?"

"Not to my knowledge, dear, though most old houses seem to have one. You mean convicts rattling their leg-irons and things like that? It has always been a happy old house, no dreadful tragedies.—Wait a minute, though; there was something, years ago in the 'twenties. It was really an accident, though the newspapers made a lot of it. Aunt Violet was so young and pretty.'

"Violet," I echoed softly.

"She was engaged to be married to some young man, they had a lovers' tiff, and she rushed out of the house, made off in his sports car, and crashed at the bottom of the drive. I was only a child at the time but I remember her body being carried up the drive on a stretcher covered by a sheet. Such a gay little thing; I can't imagine Violet haunting the place."

Later I thought it out. The point of contact. A sudden death; then, half a century later a concentration of obsessions, mine and Michael's, on Violet's particular time-slot; the old house revived to its former glory; the red sports car. An explosive situation with the stage set for a replay of the happening!

The butler's pantry with its cupboards filled with family silver; the saucer of old-fashioned plate-powder on the terrazo beside the sink, and the old telephone in the hall. And Violet's dress, the 'vintage' Vionnet.

THE TORTURES OF THE DAMNED
David Martin

You ask if I believe in ghosts. No, not what you would call *believing*. But I saw one all the same, and in this very town, what's more. The parson's ghost, we locals used to call it, which does not mean it was his own ghost.

It's the strangest thing that has happened to me in my whole life. And considering that I'll be eighty-four next week, and that I am a doctor—we doctors do see a few odd things, you know—that's quite a statement. Strange? It was terrifying! Even now I hardly ever speak of it, yet there is really no reason why it shouldn't be told. Father Rackham, bless his remarkable soul, has been dead these many years and he is the only one who might have objected.

Rackham was the rector of St Jude's. You can see his memorial tablet under the window that shows the Gospellers. A bachelor of bachelors he was. One of those old-fashioned, uncompromising, tough, earthy Christians. Hard as a temperance bun but a true and tried pastor. With the talent and energy he had he might have risen high, but he was not ambitious. When I first came here, newly married and still pretty green and brash, he can't have been much younger than I am now. He was as much a part of St Jude's as the tower itself. A spiritual fixture.

In my view he would have done well to retire. His health was failing, his cough was a proper churchyarder. What little light comes in through our stained glass windows shone through him as through a lampshade. The Reverend Albert Rackham was a sick man indeed. Did he know he wasn't long for this world? Yes, and as it turned out that was a matter of some importance.

Keep in mind how long ago this was. Today, no doubt, they have ways of putting a reluctant old cleric out to grass; by the same token, few Anglican congregations would put up with him at all, nowadays. He'd always been stern, almost ruthless; except you can't really say that about a man of God. Unbending, then. He was no hell-ranter. He simply told us straight to our faces what a mean, selfish, paganized, lazy lot we were. Which of us who had godchildren took the trouble to guide them in the path of the Lord? How many of our confirmation youngsters were given a good example in their homes? When had we last rebuked a blasphemer? But he also showed himself no mercy, coughing and wheezing his way through his long sermons.

My impression was that his flock loved him. And so it should have, for he would have let himself be flayed alive for the lowliest in his keep. Rain or hail, night or day, he did more than his ample duty. Chairman of the Benevolent Committee, prison chaplain, Poor Relief Guardian ... a fierce-hearted saint. Most Sundays his church was packed, which it scarcely is now.

For a man of my scientific training it was all perhaps a trifle too strong, but even I went fairly regularly to his services. Why? Because I respected him. He fascinated me. That weightless body, those burning eyes, his passionate preaching: such men are always rare. I won't deny that I felt his spell, which does not mean I had premonitions. But because I did attend quite often, I was there—it was the first Sunday in Lent—when all this began, and so I became a witness.

The pews were full and everything was taking its

customary course. Father Rackham, in his black cassock, was officiating as usual. But just as he was beginning to read the Lesson he suddenly stopped. Yes—his words drifted away as if he were listening to an interruption which he alone could hear. He lifted his head and then he raised his arms, both of them, as you do to ward off a blow. It was an uncomfortably warm day and the door of the church stood open, but only a very little, and he fixed his gaze on it: such an anxious, troubled, unhappy gaze! It was so intense that my wife and I, with one accord, turned in the direction he was staring. For a second I imagined I could make out a figure, but I quickly realized it was nothing, some fancied shadow, a mere trick of the light. But Rackham ... The worst was that it went on and on. He raised himself up to see better. At last he made a movement, a kind of waving away ... it was embarrassing. But nothing lasts for ever. He closed his eyes and when he opened them again the vision, if it was a vision, had disappeared and he continued where he had left off.

He still looked deathly pale when we filed out to shake hands with him on the porch. When he took mine he gave me an apologetic little smile; rather heartbreaking because it was so unlike him.

A few Sundays later it happened again. He was then getting to the end of his sermon. This time, however, it was plain that he was scared out of his wits. He was staring at a spot in the aisle about halfway to the transept. That's to say at first he was, but then you got the idea—it was eerie!—that whatever he was seeing there was advancing on him, step by slow step. He shrank back. He actually cowered. He was trembling so much, I thought he would faint: I was wondering whether I shouldn't go to him. He did not seem to know that he still had a congregation. Then he said a few words none of us could make sense of. It was very pitiful.

Later on, outside, I managed to ask him how he felt. You should have seen the terror in his face when he thanked me and murmured that he was fine.

Naturally, it made everybody uneasy. There was a deal of talk, but most people merely thought the man was worn out. It would have died down, I guess, because the next few weeks passed off without anything untoward. But, sad to say, events soon took a new and rather grim turn. As it happened my wife was there and she told me about it.

They were burying an old fellow, an odd-job gardener who had done pruning work for us, and Hermione felt she should pay him her last respects. It was a bright, sunny morning; one of those perfect ones you get in these hills.

The old boy's daughter had just cast her handful of earth—it was heard clattering on the coffin—and Rackham had said the prayer: ashes to ashes, dust to dust. He was reciting that lovely passage which is like poetry: *"I heard a voice from heaven, saying unto me, Write, From henceforth blessed are the dead which die in the Lord: even so saith the spirit, for they rest from their labours."*

Rackham, at this instant, lifted up his eyes and looked across the pit. Hermione said he must have been staring into the mouth of hell. He swayed, and if the undertaker had not gripped his elbow he would have fallen into the grave. His face distorted in anguish, he flung out his arms and uttered a cry—it sounded like *Ettio, Ettio.* His prayer-book dropped to the ground. The gardener's daughter was deeply upset; so were many others. Hermione, always charitable, was wondering whether it might not have been the name of some being that had once been close to our poor old parson, someone he had loved and who had passed away. I didn't see it like that. It is one thing to cry a name, a child's or a man's, in bitter grief, and quite another to behave as if he were standing there, an apparition, a ghost.

I was more nearly right than she was. Before night the

whole town was buzzing like a beehive and I had bottomed on what I thought was the truth of it. I got it from our midwife, whose uncle was one of our ancient identities; it had been long before her time and mine.

Who was this 'Ettio'—a fiction? No, he had existed, all right.

His name was Atyeo, James Atyeo. He was a Cornishman, a day labourer, who lived in these parts when Father Rackham was inducted. He had drifted in from the high plains and built himself a rough hut somewhere near Battery Creek. He was a lone man, had no family or friends, was a good worker and apparently did not drink. A short, stocky, dark-bearded fellow, and rather humble, so it was remembered. He was about thirty and had most of his life still before him. Then one day he was found hanging in his hut, dangling from a rope.

Because he was an outsider, a stranger, it did not cause a great stir. We've always had a big Mental Hospital here and suicides have never been infrequent. Only a handful of people still knew about Atyeo, and their memories were vague.

But something sorrowful happened now. The common judgement was that Rackham had given himself away. Perhaps he had had something to do with the chap's death! "Ettio, Ettio," became a winged word, but not spoken with compassion. Rackham's outcry was winnowed and sieved. The townsfolk divided into factions. The larger was made up of people who were sincerely sorry for the rector and, like myself, would have liked to help him. But how do you discuss such a thing with a hard-willed old clergyman? But others—it's hateful to admit—*gloated*. Suddenly I understood that Rackham had his enemies after all, men and women who all along had resented the sharpness of his tongue. Oh, there was a sprinkling of those even amongst his congregants.

No one really knew what to do. It was obvious that what

6

was hounding him refused to give him quarter, though he fought desperately to control it ... or to control himself. But right in the middle of a sermon he would still start up like a creature pursued and stare, stare, stare ... And the funerals, they remained difficult. We had individuals who, in the wickedness of their hearts, would go out to the cemetery simply so that they might relish his terror. Ghouls! Shuffling along, walking to the graveside in front of the coffin, he must have suffered the tortures of the damned.

The churchwardens were still debating whether they should speak to the Bishop, when, in the fifth month, at Michaelmas, it was taken out of their hands. Once again I was there and once again I saw it.

Evensong was nearly over. Father Rackham was facing the nave. His right hand raised, he intoned the blessing. He was making the sign of the cross and was saying *"in the name of the Holy Ghost"*—and a truly appalling thing happened. He stopped dead. Covering his eyes, a choking, gasping cry was wrung from him—"No! No!"—in a voice which was barely his. And then, horrible, he stumbled and fell, right there on the altar steps. Where he lay motionless.

We carried him into the vestry. His breathing was shallow, his pulse low. I swear that when I put my face close to his I could hear him murmur, "Atyeo, Atyeo, pity, pity ...'

Did I explain that I was working in partnership with another doctor, older than me? Usually it was he who attended the rector, but there had been no consultation all that year. That particular week my colleague was away, and I resolved to intervene, if only to prevent more scandal. One vile crone was already giving out she had seen the devil, hooves and all, hovering over the priest's form. On the steps of the altar—now I ask you!

I left our friend in the care of his housekeeper, a deaf but godly old body, making her understand that I would be back in the evening.

Our rectory is a dreary structure of ochre-coloured brick, ugly enough to be sinister. It is so hemmed in by cypress trees that the sun can barely touch the chimneys. When I arrived, Rackham was sitting up, under a rug, by a low fire. I examined him thoroughly. How thin he was! His lungs and his heart ... It was one of those cases when the spirit is—temporarily—victorious over the body.

He wanted to know how long he might still have to live. I told him: not very long, but it depended on whether he would allow himself to be carefully nursed. He must immediately surrender his parish. False optimism would not have deceived him.

He replied that he knew his days were numbered. He had been pondering his coming death a good deal of late, and I remarked that I was sure the thought could not disturb a well-armed Christian like him. He smiled wanly.

"Bravely spoken! I too never expected it would disturb me, far less make me afraid. But recently there has been a change, a mortifying change. Now I am in perpetual fear and dread. In unspeakable terror! I, who am a soldier of Christ!"

I sensed how despairingly he had resisted having to make this confession. Or was he grateful the moment was at hand? He knew, unquestionably, that a secret is as safe with a doctor as with a pastor. Lowering his eyes he whispered:

"Have you ... have you ever heard of James Atyeo? Do you know who he was?"

I believe a man can be too tactful. To pretend I was a simpleton would have honoured neither of us. I said I'd heard some rumours. I knew how he had died.

"And about the inquest? The burial?"

"No."

He sighed. "It was recorded as a plain case of suicide. From Atyeo's pocket the police had taken a carefully written note. It only said he had done an evil and cruel

83

deed for which he, Atyeo, could not forgive himself, but that he hoped God in His mercy would."

We were silent. I was thinking of what he had said ... God in His mercy. With a great effort Rackham went on:

"I was only recently ordained but I had to make a decision. I had him buried in unconsecrated ground just outside our cemetery. If you like I can tell you where; it's easy to find."

"Did no one plead with you to give him Christian burial?"

"Two weatherbeaten old bushmen came to me, but their arguments had no merit. They tried to persuade me that when a person is as friendless as Atyeo, living all by himself for who knows how many years, the smallest transgression can prey on him until it becomes a burden too heavy to bear. It may be true, but why did he not come to me? People already knew that my door was open to all. The man was baptized, and what is the Church for? He was not some stricken, miserable lunatic. That would have been different. He had laid murdering hands on himself, full knowing. I had my duty. Today of course many a suicide is given an ordinary Christian burial. Times have altered—too much, I think. If the Saviour wants to forgive him He will forgive him wherever his bones lie, but I was not free to take it on myself."

"Did no one discover what he had done, what evil, what crime?"

"No, but it does not matter. It was his conscience, the satanic twist in it, which destroyed him. Therefore he had to lie in unhallowed ground."

"Did it not trouble you at all?".

"Yes and no." He paused, searching my face. "You are a physician; you know we are not masters of our sleep. Sometimes, but not often, I dreamt about James Atyeo, and they were not good dreams. If it threatened to darken a waking hour I took myself firmly in hand. Very firmly!

There is always a remedy: prayer. And so it was until ..."
Again he stopped.

"Until you began thinking about your own death," I suggested.

"Say rather: about my own soul's salvation and the forgiveness that it too will soon stand in need of."

His voice had gained strength. "You yourself were there that Sunday, last March, when I first saw his ghost. I saw it—I saw *him*—standing by the inner door of the church, looking at me with his sad brown eyes. A ghost? It was no ghost. A ghost is a vapour, a figment. A nightmare. Atyeo, when he stands and looks at me, is as solid as the last time I saw him digging with his spade. As nuggety, as obsequious. Sometimes he walks right up ... Can you see, my friend, how my hands are shaking?"

"And when I take a funeral, he stands by the edge of the grave, or by the naked coffin, and he looks at me so patiently across the open earth and my soul cries out in agony. What have I done! To what have I condemned my brother! I have cut him off from the communion of the blessed. Perhaps they were right who said that he may not have been a great evildoer. We are so weak! A little fear, a moment's panic ... But it is an evil thing for man, created in the Divine likeness, to take away his own life. I know that I am innocent. And I also know I am guilty. He gives me no peace."

"I beg your pardon, Father," I said, "but it's clear to me that it is your own conscience that is tormenting you. Why do you let it? One has heard about those skeletons in their unquiet, unconsecrated hollows. This ghost you have called up yourself."

"I was afraid you would think that. But, Doctor, you have not seen him, and I have. And I have not yet told you everything."

"You see, when he comes to me, always in my church or at a graveside, he is dressed in his working clothes, but neat and clean. His head is bare and his hands are empty. But this morning, as I gave the benediction, he was carrying something in his right hand ..."

"Please, calm yourself."

"*He was carrying a rope.* The rope with which he hanged himself."

This was why Rackham had fainted! I wished to say something encouraging. "There is no message for you in that. Let it be."

"No, no. There is a message, and it is this: that I am full of pride and vanity, full of sin, and that I must soon go where he has gone, and that he is waiting to meet me there."

"You cannot mean—in hell?"

He did not answer. "Exorcise him," I said firmly. "Command him to get behind you. Speak against him the name of the Holy Three-in-One and lay him to rest once and for all."

"That is the last name I can speak against him." ·

"I have not your knowledge and wisdom, but one thing we both have in common: we are not permitted to practise superstition. You as a priest and I as a healer: what have we to do with ghosts and demons?"

"But I tell you, this is no ghost. This is James Atyeo."

"Impossible."

"The Almighty does not know that word."

"But you have the power! Have his grave opened, disinter him and have him put in sacred ground."

"I cannot do it." It was almost a shout. "I must not and I cannot! What I did was right. To give way now, because I am a shameful coward, would be to condone a black evil. Am I to be counted among those who have not the grace and courage to say no? Do you tell me, who must soon meet his Maker, to betray my cloth?"

"If Atyeo is so relentless ..."

"He bids me do what must not be done. Silently, with a rope in his hand, he summons me to violate my holy office."

"If you obey you suffer, and if you disobey him you also suffer?"

His chin sank on to his chest. "Suffering passes but eternity lasts for ever."

I did not have it in me to tell him that it was still his pride which was punishing him. That, like James Atyeo but probably with less reason, he had built a trap for himself. That he was at war with his own faith.

"My dear Rector," I said, "what you need is a sound sleep and the right medication. We'll soon rid you of this bogle! Its home is not in your soul but in your chest."

"Then"—he tried a humorous expression, a sad failure—"then you must prescribe for me in the scientific style. But today he came with a rope. He stood below the altar, as close as you are now, and he was toying with it."

"Hmm. On my way home I shall inspect his grave."

"Look for it at the left corner of the wall, three paces this side from where it turns. Say a prayer for his repose. And, please, say one for me also."

It was already dark when I went there, but not so dark as to hide the spot. There was no mound, only a slight depression, an outline marked by a ranker growth. Someone had cut back the branches of the bush which overhung it. The Rector, perhaps? A bleak, sombre place, yet but for his warning I would not have known that a man was lying in this ground, on the wrong, the accursed side of the wall. Poor, unhappy Cornishman!

That night I sat up long after Hermione had gone to bed. I was making notes for a modest article I hoped to write for a medical journal. My small study was a splendid room to work in: to me the friendliest and most familiar in the world. I forgot time. But it must have been about midnight,

87

or a little later, when all of a sudden I became conscious of something strange, something out of the ordinary—something loathsome, in fact.

Do not expect me to describe it. It was a feeling, a sensation, vague and uncertain at first but becoming more and more oppressive, that I was not alone. There was—how shall I put it?—some other presence besides mine. I refused it notice. Was it growing chilly in my study? Then poke up the fire! Was there a clammy, encircling narrowness? Open the french windows! And above all do not give in to fancies brought on by talking about a ghost to a half-demented old man who knows his earthly time is coming to an end.

I have said that I do not believe in phantoms and unclean spirits. But *I was not alone in that room.* No one was to be seen, far less to be heard. No movement. But *I was not alone.* I, who so dislike the mysterious, I was there, at my comfortable desk, hunched over my papers, an arm's reach from my bookcase—and *I was not alone.* It frightened me to the heart. This presence, my awareness of it, was overwhelming. All about me was a living nothingness, an emptiness alive. May my worst enemy be spared such horror!

Turning up the lamp, I helped myself to a brandy. I was free to do what I wished, save be alone again with myself. I said loudly and firmly, "James Atyeo, speak if you have anything to say!" Not a rustle or a whisper answered. The unseen force and I, together 'we were entombed in my study.

I could bear the constraint no longer. Out, into the garden! A blackness and a silence, but the presence was there too. Under the fruit trees, by the rose-bed and the yew hedge. Drawing me, driving me. I wanted to scream but no scream came. If only I could grasp a meaning!

Was my own conscience hunting me now—back to Father Rackham? Did I owe him a more generous, less sceptical attention than I had been willing to give him? He was sick: he could be in danger. I must flee to him to placate this implacable void.

I ran from the garden, straight to the rectory. Gloomy as ever it hulked beneath its cypresses. When I raised the knocker to rouse the deaf housekeeper—it would need a peal of thunder!—I discovered that the door was unlocked. Unlocked and open—in the middle of the night.

The priest's room was at the end of the passage. I could distinguish a pale, greenish light. Was he still awake? His door too was open. I stumbled in ...

The room was filled with this light, alien, glimmery, yet pervasively clear. It did not come from any lamp. From a beam, from a silken cord twisted about his neck, hung a man. Father Rackham! And behind him ... Behind him and below, leaning against the wall and gazing at me with sad brown eyes, stood another man, stocky, swarthy, with a bushy beard.

From Rackham's throat came a rattling. I struck a match and blundered my way to the kitchen. I snatched up a knife and returned with it to the priest's room. His hands were dangling down and he turned a little, ever so slowly. And James Atyeo was looking at me with eyes of eternal patience. He was coiling and caressing a piece of rope.

I cut the Rector down. I took him in my arms, I laid him on his bed, did what had to be done and brought him back to life. But I knew I was cheating his grave for but a short span. He was almost strangled, and with a heart like his ... His neck was not broken.

Atyeo, from where he stood, watched me closely all the time. He stopped fondling the rope and kept very still. I for my part, when at last I was certain that Rackham would not perish on that bed, turned and cast upon the shape a look of triumph. For the briefest moment I faced him ... and then he was no longer there. And with him vanished the light. I had to strike another match and put it to the candle.

You can make of it what you will. I do not believe in the third dimension; it is against all the principles and traditions by which I live. But one fact stands like a rock: Rackham would have died that hour if I had not come to his house. By his own hand, a suicide, like Atyeo. He was saved from that. By whom? There but for the grace of God went he. The noose? I did not carry it away with me; it would have meant leaving him between one doubt and another. I hope he burnt it.

Our Rector had three more weeks to live. He lived them sweetly and with humility, and there was time for him to have the mortal remains of James Atyeo dug up and laid to his final rest in our scruffy but well-loved old boneyard. When news of the event spread, people did not make as much of it as I feared they would, since they did not know how it had come about. At first, indeed, only four were aware that it had been done: the Curate, who had been sent to us until a new rector could be appointed; the grave-digger; I, because Albert Rackham insisted on it, and of course our good priest himself. It was the last service he was ever to read.

Ah, and Hermione, bless her shade, also knew. In the end I couldn't keep it from her. The dear woman, she *did* believe in ghosts, and for a long time afterwards would not be left alone in my study after dark.

THE HAUNTED HILLS
Mavis Thorpe Clark

To this day no cattle graze on the Hills.

These rounded slopes are a line of hills on their own, running north and south from the older range that meanders east and west. They are a kind of cheeky intrusion into a very ancient earth pattern, different from the older mountains. The trees, such as remain, are not very tall, the grass thin, the ground showing clay patches.

"Cattle don't graze on them hills 'cos there ain't nothing for 'em to eat," says a local.

But he says that because he's uncertain about the Hills, himself. Why don't cattle graze there, even in daylight? When some strong-minded stockman takes a mob across their folds—invariably in daylight—why do the beasts go as fast as possible, eyes a bit wild, noses stretched forward, heads down, plainly anxious to cover the ground?

It was in the days of early settlement that the Hills got their name. The country was mostly untrodden then by white foot, or that newly-introduced animal, the horse. Black men knew it, but the black men had gone away to some other place before the white men thought to ask what was strange about the Hills.

Horsemen riding across the folds claimed they didn't notice anything, nor their horses, nor their dogs. But this was due no doubt to their attention being wholly occupied in getting themselves through. There was nearly double the rainfall then because of the mountain-ash and blue-gum that grew over a hundred metres high on the slopes of the older mountains, and the track often induced a jumping kind of gait in the horse—slip-slop, slip-slop—that forced the rider to concentrate simply on staying in the saddle.

Nevertheless, most of them would give a horse-like snort and say, "Dogs, now, they're really sensitive to anything spooky, and those hills have never raised a single hair on my dog's neck."

It all started with the first drover who set out to take a mob of cattle to the main settlement of the new colony, a hundred and ninety kilometres away. Cattle hadn't, as yet, been driven westward over the hills to market. Mainly because it had taken such a long time to discover a way through the wall-like bush, and then because the track was so bad. But this drover was eager to get his cattle sold. He needed the money.

The track had been cut by drays and horsemen and was no more than the first outline of the road that was to become the colony's main east-west highway. It was a track so difficult for men and vehicles that, on some stretches, a coach-horse could do no more than a ten-kilometre stint before being relieved. For that distance, especially in winter, the animal had to heave and strain, up to his belly often in water and mud. Some of the horses who trod this track regularly and relentlessly lost the hair and skin from their legs and underbellies. But though their eyes rolled in misery and pain, it was never recorded that they rolled in fear of the unknown.

It was the cattle that the Haunted Hills affected.

And it was that first drover, a man by the name of Jack, whose experience gave the Hills their name. Jack saw the first happening. But he was never found—or came forward, if he could—to tell what he saw.

He was taking a hundred prime head of cattle to market. Beautiful big tawny beasts, shiny and fat from the lush pastures of the new colony. He expected a good profit, not having to pay boat haulage along the hazardous southern coast, which was the way the beasts usually reached the metropolis. It pleased him, too, to think that he would be the first to blaze this cattle route.

He whistled, off and on, as he rode or walked behind his mob. His man-made music jarred the ears of the gorgeous red-and-blue mountain lowrys, who whisked up and squeaked smartly away from such an unheard-of noise. His two dogs trotted at the heels of the herd, proud in their responsibility.

Wherever the timber and scrub were sparse enough for the mob to leave the mucky coach-road, Jack drove them over the untrod terrain. Man and beast alike were thankful to be free of the red glue.

The drover had been on the track for several days when he came to the Hills. The mob began to climb the eastern slope on this harder kind of ground, the beasts flowing around and between the scattered scrub like a slow brown river, with the dogs not missing a single slow straggler. Daylight was beginning to wane and the mob went without hurry because the day's travel through rough country had been gruelling, but they went up this eastern slope willingly and docilely enough. They knew it was getting near time to halt for the night.

Jack drove his mob across the flattish ridge and far enough down the west side to have a windbreak and some shelter from the south-easterly wind that blew so cold at night. To the south, running almost at right-angles to his hill, was the heavily-forested range that, as yet, had not yielded to the axe of man.

There was no sign of a companionable coil of smoke rising from some squatter's or settler's hut. There might have been no other human in all the world but himself. Now and again he glimpsed a kangaroo or a wallaby hopping through the scrub, but the cattle took no notice. They had become used to these bush creatures.

Jack hobbled his horse, ordered his dogs to watch the

mob and built up his fire. After he'd eaten a meal of salt beef and yesterday's damper, fed the dogs chunks of kangaroo meat, and made sure there were plenty of logs handy to replenish his fire should he awake during the night, he decided to turn in. He was as tired as the mob and his dogs.

But first he took off his top jacket with its brass buttons. It was a new jacket of heavy flannel, bought specially so that he would arrive at market looking the part of the successful drover who had brought the first herd through those Hills. Then he lay down beside the fire, with his saddle-bag for a pillow, and his thick blanket and the warmth of the big fire to keep him cosy during the cold night.

When he closed his eyes the cattle were grazing or resting quietly, the dogs watching. The night was moonlit, very still. The fire and his blanket were indeed comfortable.

The next thing he knew was a great thundering noise as though the sky was falling in on him, the saddle-bag shaking under his head, and the dogs yelping. He leapt from his blanket and knew at once that the thundering was that of four times a hundred hooves. Thundering down the hill . . . thundering away from him! As though the devil himself was after them! But where was the devil? *What* was the devil?

In the darkness, coming from sleep, at first he could see nothing about him, only hear the noise. But he could see the stars, twinkling in the black sky as they had when he closed his eyes. And he knew it was midnight. He had been a bushman long enough in this country to know what the stars told of time.

Midnight and noise. His cattle stampeding madly down the west side of the Hills. Snorting in terror, thumping through the scrub, crashing through it, heedless of injury with terror hanging on to their tails.

94

He cast around for his horse, but, even in hobbles, it had managed to get far enough away to be out of sight.

He cursed and whistled his dogs. They did not answer. Doing their duty, they had gone with the herd. He began to race down the hill after his mob, hair streaming thinly behind as though he, too, had a tail, and unaware that he hadn't pulled on his jacket.

It was not yet daylight when a wild mob of about thirty beasts hurtled through the hamlet on the river bank west of the Hills.

A store and a wayside inn comprised the hamlet and the proprietors of both were already up and about. The storekeeper was milking his cow in an open bark shed alongside his store so that he would have milk and cream ready for the publican, who was expecting a coach and passengers from the metropolis shortly before dawn.

The coach left the main settlement at midnight, and the jolted and bumped passengers would be ready for a hearty breakfast of home-cured bacon, home-baked bread, and fresh milk—the only inn on all the highway offering milk to travellers, thanks to the enterprising storekeeper.

But when the thudding hooves twitched his bucket, the storekeeper left a surprised cow to rush to the track to watch the shadowy mob of deranged cattle hurtle by in the half-dark; likewise the publican.

"Come from the east—down over them Hills," said the storekeeper, mystified.

"Jack was bringing his mob through—first man to try it," said the publican. "Due 'ere later terday. You don't think ...?"

"I dunno," said the storekeeper. "Never seen beasts come down from them Hills before."

"Never been beasts through before."

"Well, they're not mine," shrugged the storekeeper.

"Nor mine," said the publican. "And that coach is due mighty soon. Hope it don't run smack-bang into that mob and turn over."

"Yer can't do nothing," said the storekeeper. "Never catch that mob on your nag, nor mine."

"No," agreed the publican; "my Dolly don't like to be hurried, nor your Sam."

The publican and the storekeeper got along very well. They were both from that district within sound of Bow Bells back in the Old Country.

Now the storekeeper returned to his cow, still standing and wondering when her master would be back, but making the most of the interruption by swallowing as much hay as she could; and then giving a sly kick to the newly-returned milker so that he was forced to feed her more fodder to keep her quiet while he finished the job. And the publican went into his kitchen to slice his bacon and get his fire going in time for the coach.

The publican liked to look after the coach and its passengers. The coaching service was only just beginning to reach into these wild unsettled parts and, being a shrewd man, he reckoned more people would come and traffic grow in volume and he would make his fortune.

So the bacon was ready and the eggs had only to be broken when the coachman's horn was heard at the bend of the road announcing the arrival of the four spanking horses, driver and passengers. Spanking horses they were, but clothed in mud that would have to be washed off in the inn's back paddock where they would rest, while the four more spanking ones waiting there would be thrust smartly into the shafts.

The publican was quick to ask if they had seen the wild cattle bolt by.

Yes, indeed, the wild cattle had been seen! Eyes rolling,

tails streaming, mouths frothing, hides flecked with foam, they had passed only wide enough of the coach for safety, and near enough for the vehicle to sway in the rushing current of air they created as they went by. One lady passenger had almost fainted at the shock of such a narrow escape from those long, vicious horns; she was quick to accept smelling-salts from a thoughtful publican.

It was nigh a week before the publican and the storekeeper put together the various other bits of the story that came past their doors. The cattle, it seemed, were stopped farther along the track by a quick-thinking squatter. And apparently happy to be stopped, happy to have their minds made up for them, as they'd obviously rattled a long way. The squatter identified them as Jack's cattle. But they were only about a third of the herd. Which surely meant, calculated the storekeeper and the publican, that Jack and two-thirds of his herd were still up there in those Hills.

Now the store-keeper and the publican were really compassionate men—it was only because Dolly and Sam were slow nags that they hadn't tried to head off the beasts themselves. They decided that between coach arrivals, which, at this time, was a matter of a couple of days at least, they would go and see what Jack was up to.

But they didn't find Jack—not a trace of his person, that is. (Nor did anyone else who took the trouble to look as they passed through the Hills.)

But they did find his camp and the black ash of his fire, and the flannel jacket with the brass buttons that he hadn't waited to put on. They even found his horse, still hobbled, half a mile from the camp, and some of the cattle, a dozen beasts or so. Dead. Strewn down the western slope of the Hills in horrible array. Staked on jagged butts of old dead trees, heads smashed in where they'd butted tree trunks in

Z

terror to escape from whatever threatened them. And the two faithful dogs trampled to death by all those hooves. But there was no sign of the rest of the cattle, not even hoof-marks.

"Rain, of course—washed 'em out," said the publican. But he didn't believe what he said. Bolting cattle left deep hoof imprints. It would take an awful lot of rain to wash those out.

Yet except for the big dead bodies, and no Jack, the countryside was peaceful in the bright sun of that early spring day.

"But there's a feeling . . ." said the publican, looking around, especially behind him.

"Yeah . . . I reckon," said the storekeeper.

"It's 'aunted, yer can tell," said the publican, his own face white as the storekeeper's.

"We'd best get out of 'ere," said the storekeeper. "Wouldn't ride through this place at night fer all the tea in China."

"They're 'aunted, these 'ere 'ills," said the publican. "'aunted."

The next drover who went through the Haunted Hills with a mob of cattle was also named Jack, an immigrant from the Highlands of Scotland. He was determined to accomplish what the first Jack had failed to do, and, because he didn't believe that hills could be haunted, he, too, camped on the western slope, almost on the same spot where Jack Number One had camped.

But because he was also a practical fellow and did not wish to lose his herd to some unknown, but, no doubt, explicable cause, he elected to take a boy with him, and have them watch the cattle all night, turn about.

Jack himself was on watch when just on midnight the

cattle began to show signs of nervousness, to look about them as though they saw something in the shadows, to twitch their ears as though they heard something out there in the darkness. Some of them to paw and scratch at the ground, others to lower those long horns as though about to charge. And suddenly—as a shot!—to take it into their heads to go. All of them. Away they went. Hell-for-leather down the slope. And Jack Number Two after them but on his horse, the boy not far behind, and the dogs, though crazily excited, still obedient.

They held the herd from breaking though they had to race with the animals and dodge the old tree-trunks and the trees. They lost a few beasts who seemed to become quite maddened by this unidentifiable and unseen threat.

Again it was a still moonlit night, and there was nought about except for a few kangaroos and wallabies and monkey-bears grunting rudely in the trees.

But Jack Number Two was whiter-faced than either the publican or storekeeper had been when, with his mob, he reached the hamlet at the side of the river.

"There was nothing to see, ye ken," he told the storekeeper and the publican. "It was the noise—like another herd galloping . . . galloping . . . galloping! Ye ken! We heard it—me an' yon lad—above the noise of our own beasts' thumping!"

"And there was no herd to see?" said the publican gravely, his eyes wide.

"No herd—I swear! Only the noise of their hooves!"

"A ghost herd. The ghosts of the herd that the first Jack lost. That's what it be! A ghost herd."

"But . . ." said the storekeeper, spreading out his hands with the open-palmed movement only the wise dare make, "but . . . what frightened the first Jack's herd? Answer me that. No beasts had been through them there hills till Jack Number One's herd went through. So there were no ghosts to frighten *them*."

Which made Jack Number Two and the storekeeper and the publican look at each other and shake their heads.

There was no doubt, the Hills were haunted.

From then on, drovers would have avoided the Hills altogether if they could. It was often eerie enough just to sleep out with a herd in country that was still new to white men, where the dingo's howl could shiver a man's stomach, and the grunt of a monkey-bear rasp down on a man's head to lift the hair on his scalp and where, just occasionally now, a black man would slither away at the white man's approach.

The Haunted Hills were to be avoided. But meat had to be got to market. The main market was that distant metropolis, and the only track, on the hoof, was over these hills. Because it was the cheapest route to market, with the beasts feeding along the way and not needing to be hand-fed, as on the coastal sailing-ships—which also had an uncomfortable habit of piling up on the nearest rock in a storm—it was plain that beasts must be driven across the Hills.

But now the drovers made sure they were never caught on those folds in the dark and hurried their mobs through. Which was no trouble at all, because the beasts were as eager to put the Hills behind them as were the drovers, even though the ghostly herd was silent during the day. Nevertheless, while the horses and the dogs found the Hills no more frightening than any other part of the route, the cattle's eyes would begin to roll at once when they entered the Haunted Hills area and, at the crack of a breaking twig, they would take off.

Then one day a stockman who had brought his herd safely through, never losing a beast—in daylight, to be

100

sure—and was having a nobbler at the inn, declared that he had hit upon the solution to the whole mystery.

"Nothing haunted about the place!" declared he, a big-boned, narrow-faced Currency Lad—a born Colonial—of New South Wales who had long boo-hooed the ghost-minded views of his counterparts from the Old Country. "I had reason to crack me whip—quite a few times—on them Hills. An' I got an answer, I tell you—a whip-crack from the opposite slope. *That*'s the reason for the whole thing. Echoes! Them beasts heard the echoes of their own hooves as they bolted. And as they ran ... the echo ran with them. As they ran faster ... it ran faster. It nearly drove 'em mad, right enough. But it was just echoes."

The storekeeper was inclined to nod his head to the Currency Lad's views, but the publican said, "Then what makes 'em start to bolt in the first place? You just tell me that—you young know-all!"

"A kangaroo jumping through their ranks,". said the Currency Lad.

"And those beasts reared with kangaroos!" said the publican, and lowered his Cockney voice, "'aunted 'ills, they be."

Then a little man with a small geological hammer and a canvas bag for specimens went through the Hills and he came back to the Inn one day and said, "There's coal in those hills ... millions of tonnes of brown coal. Enough to burn, I reckon, as long as the sun."

"You don't say," said the publican who had been putting on a bit of weight of late because he was allowing himself an extra evening nobbler, with business being so good and settlers coming in so fast, and the coach service a daily one, from both east and west. He employed a couple of rouseabouts now, but, being a compassionate fellow, he still offered smelling-salts to ladies badly jolted by the ruts and pot-holes. Not that any one of them, ever again, suffered nearly to fainting point by almost running smack-bang into a deranged herd of brown cattle.

"I do say!" said the little geologist, thumping his hammer on the counter because it had more weight than his fist. "And some of it's been on fire—the coal, I mean—millions of years ago. Burnt holes in it, underneath the ground. Made some of it hollow. With cracks and caves underneath. Very interesting. Sleeping on top at night, I heard peculiar rumbles."

"You wouldn't say . . . like hoofbeats?"

"No, I wouldn't say like hoofbeats. Rumbles. Nothing hoof-beating about rumbles. It was the air cooling in the cracks and caves in the cold of the night."

The Currency Lad had happened to be at the Inn at the time, his bushy beard and eyebrows grown thicker and bushier. "Like I said!" he cried. "Echoes!"

"An echo from hill to hill is not an echo from underground," said the storekeeper, who also happened to be present, liking to meet any travellers passing through who had aught to say about the district.

"Same thing," said the Currency Lad.

"Then," said the publican, with some sarcasm, "I expect now that you've got some backing—in a kind of way—for your echo idea, you'll camp your herd on the Hills at night, and think nought of it."

But the Currency Lad grinned and said, "What d'ye take me for—a fool!"

And the drovers—even the Currency Lad himself—continued to hurry their agitated cattle over the Haunted Hills and made sure, always, not to be caught on those slopes at close of day and forced to camp there after nightfall.

The old-timers began to drift away or die but so many

people came in to take their places that a railway was put through the area. When the workmen were making cuttings through those Hills for the lines, they would dig and dig and work hard all day, leaving a nice tidy cut ready for the morning. But when the morning came, they would often find the cutting fallen in. "These bloomin' Hills are 'aunted," they said.

More people came when the brown coal began to be used to make electricity, and houses were built on the lower slopes of the Hills. People didn't seem to notice anything haunted about them—or maybe all those people inhibited the haunting spirits—neither did the horses nor the dogs. But the cattle did.

To this day, cattle will not graze on the Haunted Hills.

ROOM 409
Nance Donkin

About four o'clock, I jacked up. Well, wouldn't you? We'd
started rather early that morning with a quick whisk
around a cathedral, then at ten thirty it was a ruined
castle—a pretty small castle, not much left of it but the
walls; and from there it was straight on to an Abbey, walls
again and roof open to the sky, piles of fallen stones
everywhere and an underground room supposed to have
been the Abbot's kitchen. Then there was a village church, not
much bigger than our back verandah, and close enough to a
Roman fort for us to get there before the end of the morning
session.

That wasn't bad and we had a jolly good lunch at the
café next door. But it still wasn't enough for Mum, who's a
dedicated history teacher, still misty-eyed and thrilled to the
back teeth about England's Past and what it means to the
rest of the world. Even after touring England by car for six
solid weeks. Dad goes along all the way with her pokings
about in history because he left England as a boy of twelve
to go with his parents to live in Australia and he's trying to
catch up on all the things he thinks he missed. But I'd had
almost enough.

At two o'clock that afternoon we were waiting on the
steps for a museum to open. It was a good one and I
reckon I learned a lot there, but after two hours I was
ready to stop. Then Dad suggested rounding off the

afternoon by visiting an old cousin and that's when I said NO THANKS! We'd seen at least six of England's Ancient Monuments in the last three days and the thought of visiting another one, even if it was human, just wasn't my scene. We'd met some of Dad's relatives already, not one of them under seventy. I knew just how this one would behave; she'd rave on and on about how Dad had grown and how much he'd changed—scarcely surprising, is it, after twenty-seven years?

We'd arrived in this latest cathedral town on our itinerary very early that same morning, and had immediately checked into a hotel. That is, Dad made sure we were booked in for the night, left two suitcases at the desk and we drove off. By four o'clock, the parents were still fresh-footed and chirpy but I was half-dead. I begged off the visit to Cousin Eleanor and said to Dad that if he would drop me off at the hotel, I'd get our key from the desk and go up to my room to have a read. He nodded, then thought perhaps he had better come in with me, to prove that I was his son and not some young Toughie trying to get a free bed or put over some crooked deal.

So we did it that way. I mean, I'm thirteen and tall and fairly good at looking after myself, but I haven't had much experience of walking into hotels on my own and asking for the room key. Dad vouched for who I was and the man on the reception desk nodded and smiled and said to excuse him, just for a few seconds. All the keys were in the Manager's office for some special inspection and he would bring them back immediately.

I walked to the door with Dad and watched him get into the car with my mother and drive off. Through the big glass doors I could see the car until it turned the next corner. Then I went across to the desk for the room key. The first man wasn't there but there was someone else on duty, a funny old boy who looked half-asleep and certainly in need of a good brush-up. He didn't seem to fit in at all

105

well with the modern decor of the place, but I got the key from him and went towards the lift.

The foyer was very bright, with red carpets and great bowls of flowers and electric lights blazing from tables and walls and ceiling. It felt rather good to be parading around there on my own; I sort of felt like a world traveller, an important one, not just a boy having a marvellous three-months - off - school - because - it - will - be - so - wonderfully - stimulating-and-educational-for-him. I wondered if I looked any different. I *felt* two metres tall ... I'd just left the Jag outside for the parking attendant to put away, and before the night was over, I might well have clinched a couple of Big International Contracts. I thought about High Finance as I walked about the foyer (by the way, dollars into pounds didn't go seem to far in England and maybe Dad would advance me a bit more); I waved my fingers around as though I were knocking the ash off the end of a fat, expensive cigar. I had a quick peek into the Smoking Room but there was nobody there who looked like a Big Time Financier waiting to meet another of the same kind, so I pressed the lift button with a casual air. There was nobody else waiting for it; I had the lift to myself. The light was just as strong in there as in the foyer—which made it all the more shocking when the lift stopped, the door opened and I walked out into complete darkness. I took a couple of steps forward before the darkness registered properly, and then I turned to get back into the lift, but it had already gone. My fingers couldn't find the press button. They couldn't even find the door.

It really was scary. It was crazy, too. I mean, three seconds ago I was in a lighted lift, thinking about important things like what I would do for the World; then suddenly there was nothing of the world left but this darkness, and me alone in it. I knew the lift must be there. It had to be there because I'd just got out of it. I knew roughly just where it was, too, but I had a feeling that I'd sensed space just beside it, maybe a staircase, and I didn't want to go crashing down a flight of stairs in the dark. I put my hand out, found a wall and groped my way along it, fingers feeling for a switch. But there didn't seem to be a switch; no lift, then no switch.

That was when the James Bond type with the Jag, the Big-Time Financier and wheeler-dealer, melted away and left a thirteen-year-old boy whose insides began to swish about like a milkshake. I fingered my way along the wall until I felt the shape of a corner and knew I must be turning into the corridor where all the bedroom doors were. But I still couldn't find a light switch and I began to feel panicky and VERY peculiar. A word which my mother used rather a lot came into my mind. *Utterly*. Until then I hadn't had any reason to think about the true meaning of the word. Now it became part of me because I was utterly alone and around me was utter darkness. Downstairs were lights and people and flowers and a bright carpet; downstairs was the memory of the Marvellous-Me game I'd been having with myself; upstairs there was just Little-Me, alone in the utterly utter blackness.

I turned and stumbled down the other side of the corridor but couldn't find a light switch there either and the thought of that open staircase I was sure was there stopped me from searching too hard for the lift. I couldn't understand why it was all dark until I realized that this floor might have been empty until we booked in, so they'd turned off the lights to save money. So here I was, groping around in the dark, scared as hell, because some stingy hotel manager wanted to save on the electricity bills. It made me really mad, but I felt sick too. How I wished I'd gone with Dad! A dreary old lady chatting away about my father's nice nature and his lovely yellow curls was a bore but it wasn't frightening. Being alone in this black, black, long, long hall was frightening. The dark was closing in on me, I could smell it; it was moving about me in waves, brushing against me, not soft like fur, but clammy.

Then came the bright idea. The room number was 409; I felt my way across to a door, and, hoping that the figures would not be just painted on, put my fingers out to find them. It took a while because my hands had started to shake, but soon I could feel hard metal shapes of numbers on the door and I stroked them carefully. The pads on the ends of my fingers throbbed as though they were electrified. Perhaps they were, because I was *seeing* through them, as I suppose blind people must. Four . . . one . . . eight . . . my fingers told me, so that meant our room would be on the opposite side and probably at the other end of the corridor as well. I smoothed my way along with my hands until I was sure the numbers were increasing, then turned and went back the other way until I had found four-nought-one.

The hall was as dark as ever, but now I wasn't quite so scared. It was more like a game, though I was still absolutely spitting mad with the hotel people for leaving a whole floor unlit. For the sake of saving that tiny bit of money on light bills they were willing to risk people breaking their necks or being scared silly! We'd been in a lot of hotels while we were travelling about and I never remembered before experiencing such silence. There had always been somebody moving around, at whatever time we were going to or from our room, a maid checking linen, maybe, a man fetching his briefcase, or children running matchbox-cars about the hall.

There had always been light; I guessed Dad would have a few strong words to say to the management about this. I said a few strong words myself, because it took much longer than I thought it would to find room 409, and when I had, I couldn't fit the confounded key into the keyhole.

There was something very wrong with that keyhole. I

108

pushed the key in harder and tried to turn it and nothing happened. I tried again and the key slipped around and around in the hole. By that time I wasn't scared any more. I was simply foaming-at-the-mouth mad! After all that stumbling around in the dark there I was, still on one side of the door crouching in pitch blackness over a keyhole that wouldn't work; knowing perfectly well that the second I got that door open, I could put a hand up to a wall switch and flood the place with light, or else just stand and look gratefully towards light coming through a window—because I knew that the room must face the street.

Suddenly the key seemed to fit properly. I must have been jamming it into the keyhole too fiercely at first. I pulled it right out and put it in very gently, and it turned quite easily.

Slowly the door began to open. The gloom was slightly less; dark cobweb-grey instead of pitch black, but all the heat I'd felt inside me a few moments ago had turned to cold. I didn't even try to step inside. I took a step back instead. The wind which came through that slightly opened doorway was icy. I knew that if I took one step forward I would fall. It was pointless to look for light coming through windows that faced the street, no use at all to put up a hand to turn on a switch. The chilled wind and a kind of damp sighing silence told me that. There was nothing there, I knew, nothing except shattered walls and broken floor beams.

The cold began to settle down over me, spreading through feet and hands and face and through to my bones. It was like an iron coat, weighing me down. I was so terrified that for a while I did not even try to move. The years of doing things on my own to prove that I could fell away. I was three, not thirteen. I was three years old and I wanted my history-mad mother; I was crying for my big father. I couldn't understand why nobody came, because I thought I was screaming like a hurt dog. But in fact my mouth was just opening and shutting with no sound coming out. The cold spread and spread and I knew that if I didn't move soon, I might just have to stay there, frozen. I pulled my feet away from the floor, forced them to turn about and staggered down the hall until I felt there was space around me which must be the area near the lift and the stairs.

In the dark I put out both hands, grabbed a staircase railing and began to inch my way down, carefully, carefully. My breathing sounded like bronchitis and my heartbeats like a kitchen clock. There was a bend in the staircase and I felt my way around it, still in complete darkness. Then I fell. I bumped down and down most painfully, because now there was no carpet to cushion the way. The steps were solid uncovered concrete and I seemed to be falling for ever, down and down and down into a cold black night.

Dad and Mother found me lying in the lighted hall by the lift on the third floor and they couldn't understand what I was talking about. Nor could the Manager, who came to find out what all the noise was about, because I had started to yell and to throw myself around.

Mother looked twice as tall and was demanding a doctor, a solicitor, a policeman, while she crouched on the floor with me. Dad was telling her to calm down and wait until the boy could explain the situation. The Manager was alarmed but dictatorial. He said that obviously, the boy had fallen and given himself a very nasty bump, must have even lost consciousness for a while and had a kind of nightmare.

"Because, Mr Jenkins," he said to my father, "he is talking a lot of rubbish. There IS no fourth floor in this hotel. We are now on the top floor, which is the third, and your room number is not 409 but 309. Check with your key."

Dad looked down at the key in his hand and nodded.

"That's right. Now, what's this all about, Rob? Surely you're a bit too old for this kind of caper!"

Mother said indignantly, patting me on the cheek and the head, "Of course it's not a caper. He's a very truthful boy."

Like a conjuror producing a nice fat rabbit from his hat, I opened my own hand and showed them the key I'd grabbed back out of the lock. "Then what's this?"

Quite clearly it was numbered 409.

Dad and Mother looked puzzled but relieved. The manager, a tall, bulky chap, looked like an outraged emu.

"I—I don't understand it," he said. "I just don't understand it. Who gave you that key?"

"The old man at the desk, a funny old boy with a lot of white hair and a dusty green coat. He seemed a bit shaky."

"Ridiculous!" The Manager was quite snappy. "Not one member of my staff fits that strange description. They are all well-trained, alert and moderately young, which means they are certainly *not* shaky and *never* dusty! Will you please come downstairs. If somebody has been playing practical jokes, then I intend to find out who it was."

There was nobody like that old man at the desk. There was just a real dishy girl at the switchboard, a pimply baggage boy not much older than me and a toffee-nosed desk clerk who said that he had never given me a key. He remembered my coming in that afternoon with my father, certainly he did. Then he had gone to the Manager's office to collect the keys and when he came back, I'd gone. He thought I must have decided to go with my father, after all. Or perhaps—well, *Australians*, he said with a smile, were well-known as practical jokers. There could be more in this than met the eye!

Dad snorted but the desk clerk hadn't finished. "Furthermore," he said, looking at me as though I was just a smear of boot-polish on the carpet, "furthermore, that is an old key. It looks like one from that boxful we found in the basement—spares from the old place."

"The old place?" my father asked sharply.

The Manager said smoothly, "The first Royal Hotel was badly bombed during the war. It was such a complete wreck that it was left as it was, made safe, of course, with hoardings around it, until money was found for rebuilding. Then it was rebuilt, years later, in courtyard style, with only three floors but with greater width. I assure you, Mr Jenkins, that we never have had a fourth floor."

"Then where in hell did this key come from?" my father demanded. "And who the hell gave it to my son? Describe him again, Rob."

Again I told my tale. "He was old, quite old, and sort of shaky. He had a terrific lot of white hair and a dark-green coat with braid on it, and the coat looked kind of dusty."

The Manager was exasperated. "And I repeat there is nobody on the staff who even *begins* to fit that description." The look he gave me suggested that the most desirable place for me would be the mincing-machine and next appearance, meat balls for breakfast!

I was thinking hard. "And one of his eyes kind of drooped—like this. His left eye, it was."

I let the lid on my left eye fall halfway down so that it quivered and I didn't try to let it look pretty. Between them, the Manager and the snooty clerk had really put my back up, so that eye-droop was quite a performance. Just to make sure they knew what I meant I screwed my chin up too, tried to give a good old twitch effect with the right eye and waggled my hands about loosely. The desk clerk turned a pale-yellow and flopped against the counter like a fish flapping in a boat.

"My Gawd! My Gawd! Uncle Jack!"

The Manager's face was not yellow, but scarlet. He shouted: "This has gone far enough. If you're in on this, this *stunt*, then you can take your notice straight away. What

112

can your Uncle Jack, if there is such a person, have to do with this?"

"*Was*, not IS!" the clerk said. "Gave me the creeps to see the boy do that. My Uncle Jack's left eye was exactly like it, used to give me the horrors. I never liked to look at him."

"So?" the manager asked.

"So, I thought you knew. Old Jack Trehaire was my uncle. He was the night porter at the old Royal."

The Manager looked suddenly interested, and quite pale; his cheeks seemed to melt and run down towards his chin. He whispered: "*That one?*"

The desk clerk whispered back.

"Yes. You remember what happened—a couple of minutes before the bomb hit he took a case up to the fourth floor. They only found his boots and a key."

He looked at the old key which was on the desk. We all looked and the clerk gulped, nodded, and said in a thread of a voice, "409."

THE GHOST OF A CALF
Sally Farrell

The children scrambled through the barbed-wire fence of the paddock and searched through the mob of grazing cows.

"Pansy, Polly, Petunia, Willow, Gloria, Honey, Star, Moonglow, Dianne . . ." said Samantha, patting the owners of these names as she passed. "Now, where on earth is Julie?"

"Probably missing again," said Red sourly, searching the cows with a practised eye. "That's what she pulled last year. Hooked it into the swamp and calved in there. Calf was dead when we found it, of course."

Samantha shivered. "I hate that swamp. I wish to goodness Dad owned it, so he could drain it or fill it in or fence it off properly."

"That's all very well. But he doesn't, so he can't. We'd better go down there and have a look for her."

The swamp was a no-man's-land at the bottom of the Murrays' Top Paddock. One end of it had once been a rubbish tip, which was bad enough, but the rest, in Samantha's opinion, was worse. Deep and dangerous, spongy and swampy. Samantha had borrowed *Girl of the Limberlost* last term from the school library, and she knew just what the Limberlost swamp was like. She couldn't understand *why* old Julie had shoved through the fence to calve there last year. She said as much to Red.

"Because she was two weeks early, I s'pose," he grunted.
"Dad and I came up to take her home to the Calving
Paddock and she wasn't here. Just like today."

He strode on faster, remembering how he had found
Julie guarding her dead bull calf last year. Dad had been
mad about the whole thing, and had hurled the calf's body
into the deepest part of the swamp. He had bought the old
cow at a sale the previous year, because she was in calf to a
good bull, and he wanted a bull calf from her.

After finding Julie, they had taken her back to run with
the milkers, but she hadn't settled down, and had soon
gone quite dry. Mr Murray had cursed his luck again and
mated her to another good bull before sending her back to
the Top Paddock. And now her calving date had come and
gone long since, and she was to go to the sale on Tuesday.

"Hurry up, Sam! It'll be tomorrow before we find her!"

"Wait a minute till I catch up, then!"

But Red turned and went on down the paddock. By the
time Samantha joined him, he was standing on the edge of
the swamp.

"Th'old so-and-so's done it again! See this wire? She's
broken in again. We'd better get on and find her."

Samantha picked her way over the tangled wire, frowned
at the sinister black water of the swamp and began to
balance her way along the old fallen tree-trunk that
spanned the boggy creek.

Red was well ahead of her, so she hurried. The swamp
steamed menacingly in the bright sunlight. She put her foot
on a slippery, rotten patch of bark and slithered forwards
on hands and knees.

"Wait!" she gasped, feeling a knot of fright in her chest.

Red paused and turned impatiently. "What's up now?
Come on, hurry up."

"I nearly fell in." Shock tingled out through her fingers
and toes and she clambered shakily to her feet. The tree
must have been a giant, once; it was fully a metre wide in

the middle. Red had reached the end of the bridge and had jumped down into the mass of blackberries and bulrushes that surrounded the swamp.

"Is she there?" Samantha's question died away in the air as Red held up a finger.

"Listen!"

They could both hear it, now, the gentle lowing with which a cow talks to her calf. Samantha slid down beside her brother, and followed him through the rushes.

"She'll be a mess if she barged through the swamp," said Red in his usual voice. "And, of course, we'll have to carry the calf home. Hullo!"

He stepped behind a bank of blackberries. Samantha peered after him; straight into the wide, blue-brown eyes of old Julie. She stared back at them distrustfully.

"Shove over," said Red, "let's have a look at this calf o' yourn." Together, they pushed the old cow aside. There was no calf. They searched along the edge of the swamp and through the undergrowth. Still no calf.

"Are you sure she had one?" asked Samantha, pushing her damp fair hair out of her eyes.

"Of course she's got one!" said Red crossly, his own hair looking redder than ever. "You heard her mooing, didn't you? And look at her udder!" He grabbed Julie's long dark tail and held it aside. "Fairly bulging with milk!"

Julie lifted a threatening hind hoof. Red let go and pushed off into the blackberries again. Samantha sat down and thought. Julie swung her head and stared at her with wide, bovine eyes.

"You know what," Samantha called in the direction of her brother. "Her eyes look awfully funny."

Red came back. "Probably getting milk fever."

"No, not that sort of funny. Funny pecu, I mean." She looked around fearfully at the sinking sun. "Let's get her home. It'll be dark soon."

"You're cuckoo," said Red. "If we don't find that calf

now, it might be dead by morning . . . if it isn't already."

"What do you mean?" Samantha shivered, although it wasn't cold.

"My dear, dumb sister," said Red. "You must be out of your pretty little head. This cow had a calf. Now she hasn't. We've looked all round for it, and now there's only one place left. The swamp." He turned away. In spite of his heavy sarcasm, he wondered if Samantha mightn't be right and they should just take Julie home. Dad would know what to do. But—*Samantha*, of all people! He would have thought his sister would firmly refuse to leave without the calf.

"Red, hadn't we better go and get Dad, and take Julie home? If it's dead anyway . . . Red!" Samantha was up and hanging anxiously on to his arm. The hills had blotted out the sun, now, and long shadows fell over the swamp. Red shook Samantha off.

"Oh . . . all *right*. We'll drive her up round the top of the creek, where it's shallower."

Slowly, and with difficulty, they both drove Julie along the edge of the swamp. She kept stopping, bellowing loudly over her shoulder, and then plodding on again. At last they reached the broken fence, drove her through, and on up the Top Paddock. The fence would have to wait for Dad and the pliers. At the gate, Red turned to Samantha.

"You run ahead and tell Dad, and I'll keep her coming."

Samantha hesitated. "Red . . . I'm sorry I was so scared down in the swamp. It was just . . ."

"Get going," said Red, giving her a little push. "You'll make *me* jumpy next!" He grinned at her, and she ran off down the track.

She was panting by the time she reached the dairy, where her father and his partner, Jim Browne, were just finishing the evening milking.

"Have you got her?" asked Geoff Murray, looking up as he scrubbed teat-cups. He noticed that Samantha was

117

breathless, but didn't comment. After all, he told himself, kids are always haring about.

"She's on her way ..." Samantha explained quickly.

"She's calved? Must be over-due to billyo!"

"Well, she's in milk, and mooing for the calf."

"In the swamp? *Again*? Okay. I'll come. Finish up, will you, Jim?" he called to his partner. "Old Julie's calved." He hung up his rubber milking-apron and followed Samantha out of the dairy and up the track.

Red and Julie were just where Samantha had left them. Red came to meet his father.

"She wouldn't come any farther," he called, as soon as they were in hearing range, "And, Dad, I think something's the matter. You won't believe this, but her udder's all gone down. She was as tight as anything when we found her— wasn't she, Sam? Now she's as flat as a pancake!"

"Not *again*, for goodness' sake!" said his father surprisingly, feeling Julie's slack udder, and wiping his muddy hand on the grass.

Red, who had his mouth open to argue, to convince, to excuse, shut it, bit his tongue and opened it again quickly. He ran a hand through his flaming hair. Even his freckles looked astonished.

"What do you mean ... again?" asked Samantha, since it was obvious that Red wasn't going to.

"That's what the old so-'n'-so did last year," said her father, wearily.

Red recovered with an effort. "I knew she went dry very quickly," he said.

"Dry! She was never even in milk! Just like now. She's going on Tuesday, anyhow, and good riddance!"

They looked at each other in the fading light.

"But the *calf*," said Samantha.

"Dead again, I reckon. Still, I'll go and have a look."

118

He looked, but found nothing. Julie spent the night in the calving paddock, with a young and flighty heifer and her calf.

Halfway through early milking the next morning, Red and Samantha arrived to feed the ten baby calves. As they carried in the empty milk buckets, their father appeared at the door.

"Just run that heifer in for me, will you, before you go home? If she's fed the calf you can take it into the barn."

Red drove the heifer into the dairy a few minutes later, in a state of great indignation.

"It's that Julie again," he said darkly. "She's full of milk and she feels as if she's been sucked, and I found her lurking in the shed."

"Bring her in," said his father, resignedly.

Red coaxed Julie out of the Calving Shed and drove her into the dairy. Jim Browne served her with a scoop of bran, and Red's father washed her udder. "She's got it this time, all right," he said, and connected a set of teat-cups to a special bucket, designed to take the colostrum, the special, thick first milk which a cow provides for her calf. He put the cups on Julie and attended to the heifer.

Then he turned back to Julie. "Finished, eh?" He switched off the vacuum and lifted the bucket. He looked puzzled. He took off the lid and peered inside. He turned to Julie and let out a roar that made the heifer jump like a startled ball.

There was no milk in the bucket and, as anyone could plainly see, none in the cow either. Red and Samantha drove her back to the Calving Paddock. On the way home, Samantha turned to her brother and said solemnly;

"Do you know what I think?" He didn't answer, so she went on: "I think we've got a ghost on the place."

"You're cuckoo," said Red automatically. Then: "*What* did you say?"

"A ghost," repeated Samantha much less confidently.

"You're nuts," said her brother, with certainty.

"No, I'm serious," said Samantha quickly, pulling a scrap of paper from her jeans pocket. "Just listen to me for a tick, and don't say anything till I'm finished." She cleared her throat and read: "Point one. Julie's calf died last year. Point two. She went back there this year. Point three. We heard her mooing to a calf, but there wasn't anything there. Point four. She was feeding something, but there's nothing for her to feed." She put the paper back in her pocket and continued: "Her teats were all wet when we took her this morning. Point five. I'm pretty sure something was following us when we bought her home last night. Point six. There's that queer look in her eyes. Point seven. I just *know*. I felt awfully queer in the swamp yesterday and again in the Calving Shed today. All cold and prickly."

"What . . . absolute . . . bosh!" said her brother.

Samantha shut up.

On Tuesday morning, after breakfast, Mr Murray loaded Julie into the back of his truck and drove her to the weekly sale. And there, thought Samantha, getting ready for school, went the last chance of solving the mystery.

Julie was bought by George Mason, a dairy farmer who lived several miles away.

"Seems like a good milker," said Mason to his wife, "Just look at that bag!"

"I wonder why Jack Murray sold her?" His wife was patting Julie. "And for chopper price, too! I hope she doesn't kick or anything."

"He wouldn't have kept her this long if she did," said Mason. "I guess she went cheap because of her age. Fresh in, too. Wonder what she had this year?"

"You'd better write and ask him." Mrs Mason gave Julie a final pat and then stood aside while she was loaded.

That night, at about eleven o'clock, Red woke up to find Samantha beside his bed, shaking him violently.

"Go away," said Red. Samantha pulled his pillow out from under him.

"What's up now?" Red sat up crossly. "Don't tell me you've been seeing ghosts again!"

"Shush, listen," said Samantha.

"I can't hear anything." Red grabbed his pillow back again and lay down.

"*Listen!*" insisted Samantha. "There's a calf bellowing."

Red sat up again to listen, one freckled hand anchoring his pillow. Now that she mentioned it, he *could* hear something. He glanced at the luminous face of his watch.

"Well, what do you want me to do about it?" he asked crossly. "That's the heifer's calf. D'you want me to go and give it a feed?"

"No, it can't be!" A thin bellow wavered in through the window.

"Go back to bed," advised Red. "*Some* people have to work hard at school in the morning." He lay down and went back to sleep.

Samantha went back into her own room and climbed into bed, shivering in the cold moonlight. Nearly midnight. Ghost time. She pulled the sheet over her head and then pushed it back, turning on to her back. At least nothing could come up behind her now. She closed her eyes. THUMP! *What was that*? Only a possum on the roof. But it was a long time before she went to sleep, and not only because of the row that the possums were making.

Promptly at eleven o'clock the next night, the noises

started up again. This time they were closer. Samantha lay stiffly in bed, feeling cold all over. Prickles like electricity ran down her back. She clenched her hands, remembering various horrible stories she had read . . . they had seemed merely grotesque, even laughable at the time, but now ... She couldn't finish the thought. It was quiet tonight . . . too quiet, but for that lonely bellowing.

"Are you all right, dear?" asked her mother next morning at breakfast. "You look pale."

"I'm okay," said Samantha, frowning at her cornflakes. "I didn't sleep too well, that's all." ·

Red shot a glance at her down the table.

"I hope you're not worried about old Julie," said her mother. "I was, a bit, when Dad decided to sell her, but she got a good home."

Samantha didn't say anything, and her mother looked worried.

The next night it was worse. The bellowing seemed to be coming from the barn, much nearer the house.

Samantha's mother kept her home from school on Friday, trying to find out what was worrying her daughter. To all her questions, Samantha answered, Yes, she was all right; No, she wasn't worried; No, she didn't feel sick; and Yes, school was fine, thank you. How could she tell her mother that she was worried by a ghost?

That night, Samantha woke up from a restless doze to see a dark figure coming in at the door. She froze, opening her mouth to scream. Then, limp with relief, she recognized her brother.

Red sat down in the chair next to her bed. "Listen,

Sam," he said quietly and matter-of-factly, "we're going to have to do something about that ghost of yours. It's keeping me awake."

"*My* ghost ... I like that! You mean you believe me? You can hear it? You—"

"Course I can hear it. How else could it keep me awake? I got sick of the noise and went up to the barn. Like Mum, I thought it was the heifer's calf, but that was fast asleep. So were all the others."

"You mean you went up there ... by yourself?"

"Course," said Red again. "Since when have I been scared of calves?"

"But it's ..."

"Calves, alive *or* dead?"

"You ... you didn't *see* it, did you?"

"No, but I heard it all right! It was yelling for Mama right by my ear! So I came to get you."

"But what can *I* do about it?"

"Well, you're good with calves. You could feed it."

"Oh, I couldn't! Anyhow, didn't you try?"

"Does it *sound* as if I fed it?" Red cocked his head as the bellow came again: the cry of a lonely calf. "Look here, Sam, you're the one that knows about these things. If you could even see it ..."

"No!" She sat up in horror.

"But look here, it's only a calf, just like any other calf. Except that it never grows up. It's lost its mum, and it's hungry. And lonely. And *noisy*, dash it!"

"But it's dead!"

"It doesn't sound too dead to me! Maybe you could quieten it, anyway. It wouldn't stop yelling for me. I did everything bar sing it lullabies!"

He looked helpless, so Samantha climbed out of bed and pulled on her jeans over her pyjamas. She stepped into her old sandshoes and, carefully numbing her thoughts, she followed Red out of the house.

"It's in there," hissed Red, pointing at the barn. They went in.

"But it's no good," said Samantha suddenly in her ordinary voice. The heifer's calf woke up and blinked her curly gold-brown eyelashes. "We're too late."

"What do you mean?" Red stared as if she was out of her mind.

"We're just too late," repeated Samantha. "It's all right now. Look! It isn't sad any more!" She turned away, tears crowding into her eyes, and a great weight lifting from her heart. "Oh, *look*, Red! Look at them!"

Red looked, puzzled. "Them?" he said. Samantha looked at him. "What's the time?" she asked, inconsequently.

"Twelve o'clock. Come on, Sam. Let's go home." Awkwardly, he offered her a handkerchief, and then led the way out of the soft darkness of the barn.

Next morning, after breakfast, there was a phone call for Mr Murray. Everyone else strained their ears, but couldn't make anything from the following conversation.

"Who was it?" asked his wife when he had hung up the telephone.

"That was George Mason, the bloke that bought old Julie," said Mr Murray, sitting down again.

"Oh? And are they having trouble with her too?" asked Red, beginning his egg.

"Well, they were. She was a queer 'un, she was. George said she bellowed all night for a few days then got sick. They got the vet, but she died last night."

"What was wrong with her?" asked Red, reaching for the salt.

"They didn't know. That's why George rang, to see if I had any ideas."

"What time did she die?" asked Samantha calmly.

"Just on midnight, George said. He and his boy were taking it in turns to keep an eye on her."

"Poor old girl," said Mrs Murray.

"Yes, it's a pity. She was a good old cow in her time, even if she didn't do too well here."

"But she's all right now," said Samantha, buttering a piece of toast. Her parents looked at her, surprised that Samantha sounded quite happy.

Red knew what she was talking about, of course. He had heard that bellowing, and he knew the facts. Facts *were* facts until disproved. Absurdly, he felt like telling someone. But you wouldn't catch him doing that, not in two centuries! Not in a million years! Red shook his head and then scratched it, He shook it again, violently, to get rid of those queer ideas. Today was Saturday and he was going fishing with Ken White. That would give him something sensible to think about. Nevertheless, he grinned across the table at Samantha. And then he turned his eggshell upside down in its cup and shattered it with one hearty bash.

THE MIRROR
George Finkel

My father is in the Navy and has to do with submarines, so he gets stationed in different places, and most times Mummy and Mike and I go with him. I'm Kate Ellis, and we've been to Malta and Scotland, Australia and Groton, Connecticut, as well as places in England.

We came home from Groton in June and went to stay with the Grandparents. This means going to church rather a lot, because Grandfather is a vicar, but we missed half a school term, which is always something. I'm nearly thirteen, and I feel quite educated enough already. At the end of July we went to Warsash, to a house called The Saltings.

It looks over Southampton Water, and you can see the Isle of Wight most days, and it looks old because it's built of stones from a house that was bombed during what oldies call the Blitz. Of course, it has new windows and doors and things. There are fruit trees in the garden, one with the most fabulous pears, and a conservatory with a grapevine, but the trees and the vine were there when the old house was still standing. Mike and I decided that when we got a dog and a cat The Saltings would be just about perfect.

We got a ginger kitten from a pet shop, but waited for the dog until Sally, the Grandparents' spaniel, had some more pups. So we settled down, and at the end of the hols I started school at Wykeham House, and Mike went as a boarder to Stubbington.

126

With moving around so much we don't have a lot of furniture. This is quite fun, because on Saturdays if Daddy was home we'd go to Fareham or somewhere looking for things for the house. There are simply thousands of places around those parts that sell old furniture.

One Saturday Daddy said at breakfast: "You know, this is rather a gloomy room. I wonder if a mirror opposite the conservatory door would brighten it a bit?"

The dining-room is a bit dark, because it only has a french window opening into the conservatory. This was at the beginning of October, and we'd eaten all the grapes, but the vine and the trees outside still had their leaves on. Even on a bright morning this makes the light in the dining-room a kind of green colour, so that it's rather like being at the bottom of an aquarium.

"I've been wondering how to brighten this room up," Mummy said. "A wall-mirror might just do it. I saw rather a nice one in Winchester the other day."

"New or secondhand?" asked Daddy. "Remember the bank-balance, old girl!"

"Oh, secondhand—but I don't think it was old enough to be antique!"

So after breakfast we went to Winchester and parked the car near the cathedral. We found the shop, but there was no mirror in the window. A bell rang as we went in, and a lady came from a room at the back.

"A wall-mirror?" she said. "There are some mirrors in the room at the back. Would you like to have a look round and see if you can find something you want?"

The back room was *fascinating*. I found an old musical-box and some armour, and the time passed like lightning. Then Daddy said: "This wouldn't be what you saw, would it, old girl?"

It was about a metre and a quarter long by a third of that deep, set in a dark mahogany frame inlaid with a pattern of lighter woods. One long edge was different to the rest, flattened as if it had been made to stand on something. The glass glowed with a soft light, like sunshine at the end of a summer afternoon. Even in that dusty back room it glowed.

"It's been the back of a chiffonier or sideboard by the look of it. It would be worth a packet if it still was! D'you like it, old girl?"

"Oh, I do! Hung opposite the french window, it would light up the whole dining-room. It's doing it's best to light this place up as it is!"

"You could be right," Daddy said. "Let's see what they want for it. Don't seem too eager. Better let me do the haggling."

So we bought the mirror, and arranged for the carrier to bring it. I had to go to the dentist the next Wednesday, which is how I came to be at home when he called.

Mr Marsh, the carrier, is rather beery, but nice, and while Mummy was getting the money to pay him I stayed and talked. Of course, he'd called before, delivering things.

"Seems odd, comin' to this house, miss," he said, looking round the hall. "'Course, I knew the old house that was here before, when I was a lad. Before your time, that would be."

"It was, just a bit," I said. "Was the old house as nice as this one?"

"I dunno that it was, miss—I don't care for old things myself. Three hundred year old it was, so they say, wi' an orchard with a wall round it." He chuckled. "Not that a wall stopped us lads gettin' th' apples!"

We both laughed. Scrumping apples is a favourite autumn pastime, and it's a known fact that apples from other people's trees taste better than those from your own.

"There are still some apple trees," I said. "I expect they're left over from the Blitz. There's a pear tree, too, and a grapevine in the conservatory."

"If one o' the trees grows an apple wi' seeds that rattle inside when it's ripe, you cherish it—best apples I ever set tooth to, they were. And cherish that grape vine, too—they do say it was planted same time as the old house were built."

Mummy came then with the money, and Mr Marsh said: "Thank you, m'am. I'll have to get it out of the crate, because Mr Slater at the shop asked me to take the crate back."

"Can you manage all right?" Mummy said. "I've got things to do, but Kate will get you anything you need."

So we went on talking about the old house while Mr Marsh drew the nails and took the top off the crate. His mother had worked at the house before she married, and he knew quite a lot about it.

"One right funny thing she did say," he told me, "an' that was that there's been no son born in the old house this last two hundred years. Passed down from mother to daughter, it has, 'stead of from father to son in the natural way o' things."

I said that was strange, all right, and wondered how they'd kept track of the generations. Then the mirror slid out of its straw wrappings, which spread all over the hall floor.

"Not to worry, miss—I brought a sack to put all that in, if you can lend me a brush to sweep it up." So I went to the broom-cupboard while he finished unwrapping the mirror.

"What happened to the family living here when the house was blitzed?" I asked as I came back.

He was staring at the back of the mirror, and did not answer for a moment. "Eh? What was that, miss?"

I asked him again. "Oh, there was no family here when the bombs came," he said. "The last one was Miss

Broughton, who lived here wi' an old auntie. But she was an officer in the Wrens, an' the house was taken over by the army. After the war she married a naval officer, an' they've got a boatyard now, Lymington way."

He was still looking at the back of the mirror. "And I suppose they've nothing but girl babies?" I asked.

"Them, miss? Not as I hear tell. Three lads they have, an' no girls at all." He was still looking at the back of the mirror.

"Is something the matter, Mr Marsh?"

"Only this mirror, miss. 'Tis the queerest thing. I'll swear this was once in the old house—an' now I bring it to the new one."

"Why do you think it's the same?"

"Something my old mother told me. It were at the back of a sideboard or some such in those days, an' she had to get help to take it off to clean behind it."

"It still might not be the same one, Mr Marsh."

"I'd take an oath it's the same. I remember her telling me as how they nearly dropped it, once, she an' one of the other girls as were in service here. I daresay that's why it made such an impression on her." He chuckled. "Old glass, wi' a goldy look to it, she said, an' a stain like the map of Ireland on the back. See—there it is!"

Sure enough, there was a brownish stain on the wooden backing, a bit bigger than my hand and shaped a bit like a map of Ireland. The wooden back was split through the stain, and you could see the brownish paint on the back of the glass.

I shivered a little bit, though it was not really cold. "Did she—your mother, Mr Marsh—say anything else about this mirror?"

He turned it to face the wall, leaning it over carefully. "Only what I've told you, miss—but she was like me—didn't like old things. I'm a bit o' a handyman, an' I've made a lot of my own things." He began to sweep the straw

130

up while I held the sack open. "An' if I don't be makin' a move an' get back to my truck, I'll never finish my round!"

Daddy hung the mirror on chains opposite the conservatory door, and at once the dining-room seemed bigger and brighter. Though the leaves were beginning to drop from the trees and the vine by this time—that might have had something to do with the better light.

Some days that October it was almost like summer, and on those days the mirror was lovely, reflecting the room and the conservatory with a soft golden light. Some days it was rather like looking into a brightly lit tunnel, and if I stood and squinted a bit I could see myself as if I was quite old, say about twenty-five. But it was different at night.

At first I did my prep in the dining-room, facing the fireplace because the light was better for my books that way. But it was strange—after the mirror was hung I got the feeling that I wasn't alone in the room, even though I was by myself. You know how it feels if you think someone is staring at you, and you turn, and someone is? It was like that, only there was nobody there.

After about a week of this I thought it might be the mirror. I kept seeing shadowy shapes out of the corner of my eye, which seemed to vanish when I looked straight at it. So I turned my back on it, and things were all right for a while. I said nothing to the parents, of course. I mean, they'd have thought I was crazy.

When I began to feel the Shapes looking at my back I nearly did tell Mummy, but then I had another idea. At Groton we'd had a shower with nylon curtains, and one of these had been cut up to make curtains for my room. I got the other out of the chest and folded it up very small into my school-case. Draped over the mirror, it stopped the feeling of Shapes looking at the back of my neck. I had to be ready to whisk it away if I heard anyone coming, but that was all right. Nothing ever happened if there was more than one person in the room.

At the end of October there was a ball at the submarine base, one of those things the parents just *had* to go to. Two Americans we had known at Groton were going, too, and came and had dinner at our house beforehand. It was very fine, with the men in their mess-kit with medals and things, and Mummy and the American lady in long frocks. I·had dinner, too, and bagged half a glass of sauterne with the roast duck.

Mrs Briggs, the daily help, was to have come to help with the dinner and sleep in the spare room, but at the last minute she didn't. One of her kids got measles—they're the kind of kids that are always getting something—so she couldn't come. That caused a bit of kerfuffle, and Mummy said she'd have to stay at home, but after a lot of talking they said I could stay by myself. I had to promise not to open the door to anyone and be careful with the gas and all that jazz. It's funny how people don't worry leaving you alone for a bit during the day but seem terrified of doing the same thing at night.

The house seemed very empty when they'd gone, so I went and began to do the washing-up. Mummy had said not to bother, but I felt like doing something, and there was simply lashings of hot water. It took a good while to do, but when I'd finished it was still not nine o'clock, far too early to go to bed.

There was nothing I wanted to see on the telly, only sport or drama, then I thought of doing my prep. Usually I don't bother on a Friday, which this was, but I wanted something to do. Anyway, there wasn't much, for the maths mistress had flu, and there were only some botany notes and a bit of French translation. I got my case and went into the dining-room.

The central heating was on but the room felt cold, so I switched on the electric fire as well. It was noisy—the wind in the trees outside sounded like high tide on a rocky shore. And draughty: the door into the conservatory rattled. I was glad I hadn't to go out. I draped the curtain over the mirror, and settled down.

Normally the dining-room was quiet, but not that night. The rattling door seemed to get louder, and the nylon over the mirror billowed in the gusts. It was hard to concentrate on my prep, to finish it and get out of the room. But at last I was able to put away my books, and then stood well to one side of the mirror to twitch off the curtain and duck out of the doorway—quick!

All the same, I did get a glimpse into it, and it was the strangest thing. It did not seem to be reflecting our dining-room at all; it was more like a window into another room. A much bigger room, with panelling halfway up the walls and plaster above, like the hall in Grandpa's vicarage.

It was warmer and quieter in the kitchen. I made myself a cup of very thick cocoa with tons of sugar and tinned milk, and took it up to bed with some apples and a book.

I think the apples were from Mr Marsh's special tree, because the seeds rattled inside, and the book was really good, about some kids in Australia in a bush fire. I went to bed, ate an apple, and read some of the book. Then I couldn't remember if I'd switched off the fire in the dining-room.

The last thing I wanted to do was to go and find out. It was just after ten, and the parents had said they would leave the ball early, so they'd probably be home by one. That meant three hours to go, and I might fall asleep and there could be a short-circuit or something and the house get burned down. There was nothing for it—I would have to go and check.

I admit I was scared. I don't know if you've ever been in a house alone at night—quite alone? It's weird! I'm not counting Rusty the kitten, but he wasn't a lot of company asleep in his basket in the kitchen. I didn't feel much braver when I collected my hockey stick from the hall, but at least the feel of it was something.

I opened the diner door. I had left the fire on. The room was quite bright with its glow, though it felt freezing. I clicked the light on and sidled round the table to switch the fire off, trying to keep from looking in the mirror.

I was a bit clumsy reaching the switch, because of the hockey stick. Then, as I straightened up, I trod on the end of my dressing-gown cord. Trying to keep my balance, I looked full in the mirror.

There was no sign of our dining-room at all! I was looking again into that much bigger room, panelled lower down with white plaster walls above. A great fire was dying down on a huge hearth, and at a massive table sat a figure with its back to me. Its head rested on one hand, and it had spilled ink or wine or something, for a dark liquid was dripping on to the floor and lying in a spreading pool.

The figure had white hair tied at the back, like in the pictures of Captain Cook, but it was splashed with something. It pressed itself up from the table, turned slowly, and came with dragging feet towards *me*—towards the mirror—but as if it wasn't there and were coming right through it. It took up a candlestick from the table, and for the first time I saw the face. And I screamed!

Because it had only half a face, with a single eye, and the blind side was a mass of tattered flesh and shattered teeth and bone. The liquid dripping to the floor was not ink or wine—it was blood.

I didn't only scream. I struck out with the hockey stick at

134

that dreadful face and the mirror shattered into a thousand bits. Then I fainted for the first time in my life.

When I came to the room was different. It seemed quite warm, and the outside noise was no more than on any other breezy night. There was broken glass all over, and I'd cut myself a bit. Seven years' bad luck, I thought, but I felt quite calm about it. Though I was glad to get out of that dining-room.

I bathed the cuts in disinfectant and put band-aids on them, after I'd gone through the house and switched on every light, even the one in the broom cupboard. I collected Rusty from his basket, snuggled him inside my dressing-gown, and took him to bed. This is not allowed by House Rules, but that night I didn't care. He purred like an electric coffee-grinder for a while, then went to sleep. I felt as if I'd never sleep again, but I did, with two lights on in the room. It was a quarter to two when the parents woke me.

I didn't care if they laughed as I told them the whole story—about the Shapes in the mirror and Mr Marsh's tale of his mother, the nylon curtain—everything. About the chill in the dining-room and switching on the fire, and going down to switch it off. And about the Face.

"Not to worry now, Kate," Mummy said. "I thought there was something queer about that mirror. *I've* seen Shapes in it, too, out of the corner of my eye."

Daddy cleared his throat. "Might as well tell you," he said. "I thought I saw a movement in that mirror myself. It worried me so much I had my eyes checked by the specialist at the base. He said they were one hundred per

135

cent all right." He turned to me. "You scuppered the thing with your hockey stick, did you?"

"I'm sorry, Daddy."

"Ah, not to worry! We'll get a do-it-yourself mirror next time, to make sure it's ghost-proof." He turned to Mummy. "What about flashing-up some coffee, old girl, while I square away the broken glass?"

Breakfast was rather late the next morning, and after it Daddy called me into the sitting-room. Under the glass top of the coffee-table was a yellowish sheet of paper with a brown stain on it, shaped rather like the map of Ireland. I'd seen a stain like that before.

"Where did this come from? It looks very old."

"It was among the bits of broken mirror," Daddy said. "I suppose it had been slipped between the backing and the glass. It's old, all right."

"How old, exactly?"

"There's a date on it—October 31st 1762—but it's not easy to read. I could take it to the Dockyard Museum, I suppose—the curator must be pretty good at this sort of thing—but I dunno."

I looked at it. The writing was spidery and shaky, and I wondered that Daddy had been able to read any of it. "What have you been able to make out, Daddy?"

"Quite a bit. The writer was the man who once owned the old house that was bombed in the war. He'd been shot, and was dying as he wrote it."

I shuddered. "How horrible!" Then Mummy came in, and we sat together on the settee.

"How did he come to be shot? Was there a war, or something?"

"He was murdered, by the look of things. It's all a bit confused, the way he wrote it—not surprisingly—but he

136

had a cousin, it seems, who not only stole money from him but also eloped with the lady the writer was going to marry. Theft was a hanging matter in those days, but nothing was done about it. The cousin came back, to try and get more money, and there was a quarrel. The writer was shot, the cousin arranged things so that it looked like suicide, and went off leaving him for dead."

"Only he wasn't dead," I said, think of what I'd seen in the mirror.

"No. You seem to have seen the victim at his last gasp."

I shuddered. Then I thought of Mr Marsh and the story about no sons being born in the house for two hundred years. "Did you read anything in the paper about a curse?"

"Now how in the world did you guess there was a curse? There is, as a matter of fact. He lays a curse on his murderer, that he shall have no male heirs—no sons, I mean—as long as the house—the old house, that is—shall stand."

"I knew it must be something like that!" I said, and then I told them about Miss Broughton-that-was and her family. "That's one bit that's come true, anyway, because the old house had been blitzed before Miss Broughton married."

"That poor soul!" said Mummy. "Robbed of his bride, then murdered to look like a suicide. You know what that meant in those days?"

"I know suicide was looked on as a crime," Daddy said.

"It was," Mummy said. "In those days a suicide was buried at a crossroads with a stake driven through him—without a burial service."

"Ugh!" I said. "And the cousin got off scot-free, except he had no son!"

Mummy leaned forward to look at the paper. "You know what I think?" she asked. "Last night was Hallowe'en—All Souls Eve. That poor soul wanted the mirror broken—he wanted that paper found!"

"He wanted revenge?" I said, not sure what she meant.

"No, Kate. Not revenge. He wanted rest and peace." She looked thoughtful. "I wonder if my father could come down for a few days?"

"Why not, old girl? But what for?"

"Because he's an ordained clergyman—a clerk in holy orders—and there's a poor soul here who's never been properly buried. We could probably find from parish records what was done with the body, and go there and say the proper service. There'd be no more trouble in this house then, I'm sure."

We did just that, burial service and all.

But what I would like to know is this—how did the paper get behind the mirror? But I suppose we never will find that out.

SAILORS' GRAVES
Sinclair Buchan

Pellets of foam showered over the deck while their parent waves went seething under the yacht. Chris strained on the tiller, cursing the craft back into the wind, but three hours of shifting wind and sea left little strength for straining. His skin was mottled and raw from the flying spray and smarted viciously as another green roller slapped over the cabin into his face. The yacht was more sluggish now, slower to come round. The sail was well-reefed, no sign of a break-out along the boom, but while the wind still blasted across the sea ridges there was a change below the surface, and the rudder wouldn't hold them on the wind.

Through the porthole in the cabin door he counted three life-jackets. Julie saw him stooping and waved reassuringly but the children didn't move. Susan's transistor radio hung on her wrist in a plastic bag. Small boats were scattered from Kangaroo Island up to Adelaide and radio warnings were calling them into shelter before the cyclone swept over the fleet. Weather reports for water craft were called every quarter-hour and Susan was copying the barometer readings on to a chart. The heeling table, the slap and rattle of water down the hull did not exist for her any more than for her younger brother. His little feet pushed on the lee boards of the forward bunk and his knuckles were white on the grab-rails as he peered out of the fore-cabin porthole looking for the birds.

139

Peter was worried about the birds. When they had nosed out of Coffin Bay at first light the gulls drifted behind them, swimming at first, then rising in white shoals as they cleared the silent fleet to wheel in noisy circles against the dawn sky. On the southward leg the gulls were overflown by occasional pelicans and shearwaters homing on to Kangaroo Island. On the run eastward through the Strait heading for Adelaide the gulls followed, waiting for Peter to throw them bread over the stern. Then they swooped and fought in rowdy combat for the sodden morsels, to his vast delight.

Crossing below the shallow gulfs lunging like spear points into the belly of the continent, they had been out of sight of land when the first gusts hit. A long low swell, at first marked only by a rocking of the masthead, built up from the south and shortened to a brisk chop, sending irritating spouts of water over the coaming and into the cockpit. The sky darkened, uniformly at first, a thin shawl of mist forming and condensing on the metal fittings, then great cauliflowers of cloud tumbled out where the cold, dry winds sweeping up from the south pushed under the warm, moist air near the land. And all the time the wind had increased, whining through the stays and sails. The waves lengthened again but struck as fast as the shorter chop until their tops were sheared off by the wind and hurled in great sheets of spray across the surface. When the sails no longer cast shadows, Chris had called his wife and Susan to help him shorten sail, leaving Peter by the wheel wailing that the birds had disappeared.

The tide seemed to turn on them then and it was wind against current, the seas slamming into the side and thundering over the rail. Julie had taken the children into the cabin, Peter crying for his beloved birds, just before a hanging wave crashed on to the deck. It snapped a boom guy and sent it curling into the cockpit. Chris moved to close all sails down but another wave slammed over them and

140

there was a popping of wires and a splintering of wood. The yacht heeled upright and the broken mast and rigging sawed along the lee rail till the drag of wind and wave snapped the last fibres, leaving them a hulk on a still-rising sea.

The tips of the steep waves shed needles of water like sparks from an anvil, and the horizon was a ragged rim of water only a hundred yards away. Chris shortened his safety line and crouched against the cabin where he could see the compass card and align the stub of the mast against the flying scud. Once, as the yacht laboured up out of a foaming trough, the bow caught in the wind, broached beam-on and slid sickenly over the crest. The next comber seemed to fall on the hull and when it passed the wheel spun uselessly, a boom lashing carried away and the compass smashed. He had to move back where he could reach the tiller. More waves tossed them across the broken surface like a piece of garbage before he brought the nose into the wind again and it became a grim wrestling match to stop the yacht twisting on the crests. The only thing that mattered was staying afloat, and that meant keeping the bow into wind and sea.

But now a new dimension was developing. The hull was still heeling-and-toeing and the spray still bursting in clouds off the foredeck but a slow dangling swing of the loose boom built up and spoke of a change in the sea current. Through the door glass he caught a glimpse of Susan moving to the barometer, then Julie looked out, mouthing something to him. The waves were too high to risk leaving the tiller and he beckoned her out to join him.

She grabbed his arm and pulled herself close. "Chris, the glass is falling faster. Susan says she's never heard of such low pressures."

"We must be coming into the eye of the cyclone. Things should calm down then and maybe we can find some shelter before we have to fight our way out the other side."

His throat was hoarse already from shouting to be heard above the howling wind, and he motioned her to take the tiller.

"But where are we?"

He reached for the flailing boom and lashed it short. "No idea. The compass is broken and the wind has probably shifted. Our hope is for the sun to come through soon. How are the kids?"

"Susan's all right, head down in isobars and tide-tables. Peter can't think of anything but his blessed birds." Julie laughed in a tone pitched near to hysteria.

He grasped her hands and pulled her close. "There's sure to be a lull soon, but we might have to abandon the yacht. Go and check the life-jackets again."

Julie pulled herself across the cockpit and back into the cabin whilst her husband wedged himself against the coaming and looked astern. The wind seemed to have slackened a little, the sea was not so broken and the grey walls closing them in had receded a little. Forward, along the side of the deckhouse, spray still spurted skywards with each passing wave but it was not blasting him with salt darts any longer, and there was a darker line appearing where sea and sky were separating. But the clouds still merged in a continuous overcast and there were no shadows to give him direction. As the wind decreased, the sea settled to a march of gigantic but predictable rollers. In three hours, through compass failure, he had lost all idea of direction or position. The yacht was still afloat, but wouldn't stand another bout with the cyclone. The pop music on the radio died away and a voice began another weather warning.

"Daddy! Daddy!" Peter's shrill cries tailed off and he dived for the cabin to jump back as the little boy dashed into the cockpit. "Look, the birds, the birds are back!"

They were coming in their hundreds, breaking out of the misty curtain, glissading over the crests and upturning their wings to skid into the water. White, darting gulls, black cormorants, pelicans like sombre bishops, they bobbed gently on the swell around the yacht. Petrels and black ducks skittered into fussy landings with feet braced and tiny wings flapping frantically, and even occasional penguins bobbed out of the depths. The surface seethed with birds. The gulls paddled to maintain station among themselves but the pelicans, great grey galleons of gloom, sat motionless, as if waiting for something.

A brown ball of feathers skimmed low across the wave tops, struck the mast stub and tumbled along the deck. Julie picked up the stunned shearwater and nursed it until she could no longer stand Peter's pleading. He cuddled the shivering bundle and ran round the cockpit in delight, calling to the other birds and scattering pieces of bread among them. But they ignored his cries and rocked like ships at anchor on a running tide, huddling against the wind.

Julie called that the barometer was still falling. Chris could sense that himself, the way the feathers ruffled on the gulls and the sea surface seemed to swell as if drawn upwards, and he looked around uneasily in the silence. There was nothing to see but the bright, white curtain with the birds crowding up to it like a million footlights. The wind dropped suddenly. A lightning flash leapt down to the sea, with immediate thunder.

The children, Peter crying, joined them in the cockpit and Susan, pale-faced, looked uneasily at the white shroud around them. "Dad, the glass is still falling. What do you suppose is happening?"

Chris pushed his hair back and it crackled in his fingers like nylon. "Electricity. The air is alive with it."

Another salvo of lightning blasted over them and with it came a smell of bitter burning. The music stopped and the radio died in momentary silence, then a slow burred voice, indistinct at first, came through.

"It is of no more use. We see no thing of theirs."

"Susan," her father shouted angrily. "Don't change the radio. We need those weather calls."

"I didn't touch anything. It must be the programme." The girl was trembling with fright. She gave a little sob, pushed back against the coaming and pointed.

Where the birds were thickest, high on the swelling sea, was a boat.

It was an unusual boat, pointed fore and aft. Another lightning flash showed a man in a dark-blue coat near one end, and another in a grey smock facing forward and wielding oars in a slow motion. The current was bringing them closer, but neither man seemed to notice the yacht.

"There is no sign, Commander." The voice this time was reedy and sharp. *"The wrack of the pinnace I found near here."*

"But no men, Mr Fowler, no men."

The voices from the radio seemed to match the gestures of the men in the boat, now drifting among the birds only yards away. Peter buried his face against his mother and Chris moved towards Susan and the radio, but Julie spoke crisply, peremptorily, her eyes on the drifting boat. "Quiet, all of you."

"Eight men, Mr Fowler. And Thistle among them, the best master I knew."

"A good master, Commander, that's true."

"Aye, and Mr Taylor, a midshipman amiable in manners and temper."

The figure in the blue coat nodded to the words.

"And like Thistle, Mr Taylor was practised in astronomy and useful in the survey work."

"To upset in a ripple of water. Thistle, who weathered worse shores in a whaleboat with Mr Bass."

"It was a ripple to test any sailor, Commander. In the search I was near to upset when the tide had ceased to run."

144

"We have seen many strong ripplings and waters uncommon smooth, too, as now."

A pelican, like a black-and-white carving, drifted between the two boats in slow gyrations.

"The tides set fast to the northward here. It may be the sea does run to Carpentaria and we shall come to Port Jackson by Endeavour's Reef."

"The tides are setting and will run fast to sou' sou' west, Commander. We have come ten miles along this shore, followed each sinuosity of coast and found only a small keg of Mr Thistle's."

"It is a strange unknown coast, Mr Fowler. The compass varies and not always by the iron in the ship. It may be there is iron in the country, or the islands hereabout."

Julie took the chart from Susan's limp fingers and looked at it thoughtfully as the soft voice spoke again.

"Keep the rough chart before you, Mr Fowler, as we run back by the tide. I fear there is upsetting weather to come. There are no birds, when yesterday they were all about the ship."

The water around the boats was like glass, the birds twisting slowly on the eddies. There was no sign of land or sky for reference, but there was a sensation of movement, of a change of heading, of a slow settling to a course and of being in the grip of a current. The other boat kept station twenty metres away; both craft slowly lined up on the same heading. A soft curtain of rain drifted over them. Then the birds came to sudden life, the pelicans shaking great heads and the gulls their grey wings as the shower speckled the water. There was no air movement: Chris realized the current was carrying them through the rain. The sea surface was grey like old pewter; the birds rested on it like toys on a mirror. Peter forgot his fears and stood by the splintered wheel calling to them. The rain had vanished utterly into the haze that hung over them like a white tent and a pelican, etched in sharp sepia, disappeared into it to emerge again with a few leisured strokes.

Julie touched her husband's arm and pointed. The haze was thinning and a dim smudge appeared as though drawn with charcoal across the horizon. The island was suddenly clear, not floating in the sky any more, but a hard-backed reef thrusting out of the water. He tried to estimate its size and distance, but any guess was as good or bad as another. All he could tell was that they were in the grip of a fast current and moving away from it. There was a movement in the other boat.

"These men shall have their headstones, Mr Fowler, more cared for than by any Boston Church. Thistle's Island I have placed already, and this—" The blue-sleeved arm pointed at the receding island. *"This shall be named for Mr Taylor."*

"I have it marked, Commander." Fowler's voice was faint as he bent over a chart board.

Julie and Susan excitedly stretched the chart over the cabin roof and looked intently at the Commander.

Fowler's reedy voice came stronger again. *"And what of the ripplings where they upset? These should be shown for warnings."*

"Aye, but not for men. I would not name for memory what brought a man to drown. There are more islands down our passage to the ship. I will call them for the six and you may mark them as we go."

The haze was lifting and drawing away, and under it the light was pale and cold. Suddenly there was a calling and clattering of wings as the birds began to take off. The peppered surface became a boiling cauldron as gulls lifted easily and wheeled in short arcs, orange feet tucking up into white bellies, to join an overtaking flock. The pelicans, awkward and noisy, paddled to face the same way and began their lumbering runs, wings and feet pummelling the surface till they, too, were off and veering away, leaving the sea empty except for the two boats.

"Grindal's shall be the next." The arm pointed to a brown hump away to port.

"Dad." Susan was sobbing with excitement. "Grindal's Island is here on the chart, and look! Here's Taylor's Island!"

Julie ran a trembling finger down a coastline; there was a choke in her voice, too. "We must be running on the tide out of Spencer Gulf, and only about three kilometres from shore."

Ahead there was a slow darkening but nothing they could distinguish. Overhead a gull screamed, distant and insubstantial, and then came a sound that Chris dreaded, a fresh slap of water and a heeling of the hull to starboard as a gust of wind rolled over the sea.

"Little shall have this stone, Mr Fowler." The Commander pointed through a swirling uplift of haze away to port where another brown stump of land stirred out of a seething sea, and the cyclone was on them again. Before visibility closed in, Julie took a rough bearing on it and back to Grindal, now almost directly astern.

"We're being carried too close to shore," she said uneasily. "And Lewis Island is somewhere between us and open water."

"Commander, I see the ship full ahead in the cove." Fowler's voice faded then came back strongly. *"There are islands again through the ripplings towards Thistle's."*

"Aye, Thistle." The Commander's voice was despondent. *"A sailor before the mast—now an officer drowned. Name Lewis and Hopkins as stepping-stones to Thistle."* He pointed ahead over the steep white chop. *"And this, our anchorage of memory—"*

The deep voice died away on the rising wind. There was a burst of radio static. A darker patch appeared in front of them and away to starboard, parallel to their heading, a line of white water. Chris flung himself on the tiller but there was no response; the yacht surged on between the smaller boat and a spine of breakers like the teeth of a saw. The wind was still rising, roaring over the yacht and hurling great sheets of water across the cockpit. The darkening was still ahead and the fog lifted farther to show the breakers curling around in front where a yellow beach stretched across their path under a green upland.

Chris shouted to his wife to check the children's life-jackets again. The deckhouse was being spattered with spray whipped off the tops of the combers by the wind now driving them straight into the little cove. "We'll have to go overboard when she beaches. I'll take Peter. You and Susan stay together."

A flap of sail bellied up on the boom from a slipping rope and rattled in the spray. They were in broken water now; leaving the tiller Chris hoisted Peter and held him forward against the rear of the cabin. The waves were higher and steeper and the hull lifted lightly on a curling crest, swung almost broadside then spun into the line of surf and surged forward like a steeplechaser.

The boom shivered as the yacht struck. Splinters flew from the shattered mast, a following wave rolled her forward over the embedded keel until they looked down the submerged bow into an unbroken expanse of surf. Chris squeezed Peter against the coaming as the radio, in its plastic bag, floated out of the cabin and washed along the deck. From the raised cockpit he saw his wife and daughter fight their way, arms linked, down the deck and strike out towards a ring of white water encircling the other boat. Then another wave piled over the stern, twisting the hull and rolling it sideways. He grabbed his son in one arm and pushed into the tormented sea.

They hung for a moment in the backwash before the next wave lifted them and rolled them down its face like logs.

He could hear Peter choking for air and lunged down with his feet to get a grip on the bottom. The wave washed back again; his boots sank into the racing sand and he leaned against the drag, holding the boy away from him to help his balance. Then the breakers engulfed them again and he fought against the undertow until a larger wave threw them out where the sea ended and the beach was hard. He pulled his son over his back and crawled higher up the sand until he came to dry seaweed and knew they were safe. He turned to look for Julie and Susan, but fell forward exhausted.

"Chris, Chris!" Julie's voice was urgent and shrill, and her fingers were kneading at his face. The stabbing pain went out of his throat slowly and he sat up.

"Susan—Peter, where are they?"

"They're all right. Better than we are."

"The other boat, is it—?"

"It's gone. Oh, Chris, it just disappeared." Her voice rose again. "But come with me. You must, you must."

She helped him to his feet and half-dragged him forward up the dunes to where Susan stood beside a stout post with a plate fixed to it.

"Look." She whispered. "Look at what it says—"

MEMORY COVE
His Majesty's ship Investigator
Matthew Flinders, Commander
anchored here Feb 22, 1802
Mr John Thistle—the Master
Mr William Taylor—Midshipman
and
six of the crew were most unfortunately drowned near this place from being upset in a boat.
The wreck of the boat was found, but their bodies were not recovered.
NAUTICI CAVETE!

He read it through again, aloud, and as he spoke a small

149

hand crept into his, and he looked down at Peter. The boy's fair hair was plastered over his scalp like wet string, but he was staring back towards the beach with a blissful smile on his salty face. With tiny fingers he opened his life-jacket and tenderly lifted out a sodden shearwater. He put it carefully on the dune grass and watched it wobble down the sand. The beach was not yellow any more. It was cobbled in white and grey with an occasional black fleck where a pelican obtruded among the gulls. The only thing moving was the unsteady shearwater, until it merged with a thousand other silent seabirds, feathers sleeked down by the wind, facing out to the yacht dying in the high, bright waves and the sailors' graves beyond.

THE WOMAN OF LABU
Olaf Ruhen

The light from the torch of coconut fronds in Biria's left
hand illumined the water that lay within the range of her
upraised spear, that caressed her body up to her waist, that
sheltered the fish she was hunting. The light swelled and
diminished, but within its protection this only was her
world, the water, and the sand beneath her feet, the velvet
air of night and her spear-armed self; and the things that
lay beyond the night lay also beyond her consciousness.
Not quite all, for the other woman was in her thoughts, the
woman Ingat who at this moment was likewise waist-deep
in water, armed likewise with a spear and a blazing torch.
Biria had only to lift her eyes to see the whereabouts of
Ingat, the little woman; but she kept her concentration for
the little world illumined by her torch, and the Ingat of her
thoughts was an intruder in that world.

Two fish swam lazily into the compass of the light, two
good fish, and one for the taking. The woman Biria, alert
before, now poised upon the brink of integrated action, the
torch in her left hand continuing to rise to its zenith with
the controlled lifting of her arm. In her right hand the
upraised spear was vibrant with readiness, yet her tensed
muscles were so controlled there was no alteration in the
rhythm of the water droplets sliding steady from its circlet
of points.

For a moment she seemed to regard the fish with

151

dispassion; and when she moved again her spear hand never quivered, but the blazing torch dropped swiftly and steadily almost to the water, its combustion strengthened by the movement, and its light confined.

When she stilled the torch the flame surged up, fat and rich once more, and in the sudden accession of light the fish were clearly to be seen, and her muscles loosened into a song of movement, and the spear thrust straight and true, and took the fatter, heavier fish upon its points. Torch in one hand, fish-bearing spear in the other, Biria turned and waded back through the little surf to walk to the big fire higher up the beach. When she turned, the little woman Ingat turned too, and came running with her torch and her empty spear.

"Oo-oo," she called. "He's a beauty. You have the eye for the fish. Three already! And I have none."

Thus and thus she always chattered, skipping sideways, careless of her torch and scattering sputtering brands along the beach, bright-eyed and noisy, and admiring the fish the like of which she saw every week of her life.

"Fish won't come on your spear by themselves," Biria snapped. "You can't catch fish on the beach here, out of the water."

Ingat was always the same, she thought. Ingat did little work, and what she did was not well done. The taking of fish was a game for her, all her tasks were games and all her days a happiness. Ingat scamped the work of a woman, and yet Ingat was well loved. Everyone had a smile for her; everyone stopped at her house for a word and a gossip, and shared good luck with her.

Some of the people were at the fire, the fishermen replenishing their torches, and others bringing wood, or stringing their fish, or just gossiping for the night's company. The firelit air carried a staccato of voices that ceased briefly while the people eyed the fish on Biria's spear; and then burst out again, mingling with the other

152

sounds of the night, the frogs and the insects and the wood snapping in the heat. Beyond the influence of the firelight the beach stretched wide and white, darkening only under the shade of the trees, and by contrast, where the dancing pathway to the moon angled away from its edge, and went for ever over the dark and dancing water.

Past the lines of the surf, for the full length of the beach, the bom-bom torches rose and fell, rose and fell, accenting the rhythm of the search; and with the movement each rubied light swelled and diminished, contracting to a spark-shedding minimum with movement, and expanding to a great orb of fresh-fed flame in the momentary halt above the water's surface.

And in this moment of light, if the fisherman was nearby, you could see his body lit red and defiant against the glinting water, a brief vision of the hunter that in a second faded into a mass that was more of the mind than of the eye. Sometimes the fisher was a woman, and sometimes there was a glimpse of beauty as the light struck the upraised spear arm, the lifted breast beneath it, and the wet lap-lap swathed low on the belly.

Biria strung her fish with the others she had caught, and stooped to take a dry lap-lap from her billum, the head-net she wore wherever she went; but Ingat protested, loving the night and the movement of the night, and loath to go to the next experience.

"Once more," she cried. "Just once more. I haven't caught a fish."

Biria stopped, unwilling, her hand on the open billum, her firm programme questioned; and Ingat began to plead.

"All right," said Biria; and already Ingat was running back to the gentle surf. Biria took a new torch, ready bound to hand, and lighted it at the fire and followed. Within minutes Ingat speared a little fish, and she laughed and called out, shouting and showing it to everyone, bragging like a little girl with her first skirt, although the

153

fish was smaller than any of the three that had fallen to Biria. And Biria noted, sourly, that people paid attention too, and made jokes about little Ingat and her little fish. She was irritated, yet even while she felt this she wondered about herself, that Ingat, so friendly, and so rich in friends, should seek her company.

While they dressed, casually folding clean dry lap-laps over the wet ones, then slipping these away from underneath, she envied the figured cloth that Ingat kept for best, yet wore to the fishing. And her envy grew as Ingat, following a fashion new to the place, took a flower-patterned scarf and tied it about her neck so that her little breasts lay half-concealed within the bight of the cloth; for Biria had no such clothing.

When they were ready they wrapped the fish in taro leaves and placed them with their wet lap-laps in their corded billums, and swung the carrying straps to their foreheads, and went on their way. Biria was from the village of Labu, and Ingat from a smaller place in the hills beyond, so that their paths ran only a little way together before they separated. They talked awhile at this place of parting and Ingat said, "Not tomorrow, but the next day we will come to bom-bom the fish again. The moon is so big it is a shame to waste it."

They agreed on this, and Ingat said, "We'll meet here where the paths join, late in the afternoon, and walk together to the beach."

When she was away from Ingat, walking by herself on the bush path, Biria wondered why she had agreed. She felt no love for Ingat except when she was with her, but Ingat was her only friend, the only woman who sought her company. The rest, the women of her own village, only tolerated her. Sometimes she said hard things about Ingat, the useless woman, tiny and slight, and lazy as well. But when they were together Ingat made her happy, and sometimes they laughed together like children. There was no woman in Labu with whom she laughed.

The responsibility of meeting Ingat became a little burden in her mind, something useless to carry, and she wished she had not assented to the arrangement, but when the time came she was first at the junction of the paths, and she waited, but there was no sign of the little woman.

She sat for a long time; then because she was a woman who must ever have something to do, she went into a high place above the track and looked for frogs.

She found three good frogs and put them in her billum to take home to her family. Then she returned to the path but Ingat had not arrived.

"The woman must be dead," she thought. "Good enough for her."

She waited and waited, and it was nearly dark. As the wind died she heard the thin sound of a sing-sing, a far-away wailing that seemed to come from the village in the hills. She listened hard to try to make out the nature of the sing-sing, but the sound was too tenuous. It lay right at the very bounds of her hearing, so that the lift of the wind blotted it out, and the surge of the larger waves on the beach destroyed it.

"Ingat has died," she thought, "and this is the sing-sing for her death.

"I wonder," she thought, "just what was the manner of her dying."

And she thought of Ingat, the little woman, lying dead, her bubbling life still as a stone, and she became filled with sorrow.

"She was a good woman, though she worked little. She was my one good friend," she thought. And she began to rock herself backward and forward as she waited, squatting at the junction of the paths, but just at that time she heard something and looked up to see Ingat coming along the path; and immediately she was angry because Ingat was there, and was herself, and had not changed.

"They're making a sing-sing in your village," she said. "Why?"

"Oh, they make a sing-sing about nothing," Ingat answered lightly, and immediately she asked, "Have you waited long for me?"

Biria asked no more questions, but she thought this a strange thing that Ingat should not talk of the sing-sing. It could have been anything, it could have been nothing. But from what she had been able to hear, Biria thought the people had been singing a death.

However, they went together a little way along the path, and there was a place where they set a fire and cooked themselves some taro. Biria did most of the work while Ingat talked, and told all the gossip of the village. Once Biria lifted her head and said, "I hear a sing-sing. Surely there must be a sing-sing in your village"; but Ingat hardly glanced into the gathering dark, hardly stilled her busy tongue for a moment; and then she said, "I hear nothing."

And she went on with her tale of young Maiu, and how he was believed to have consummated an attachment he had for the wife of Animari, the headman, and how their place of assignation was beneath the floor of Animari's hut so that the lovers would be warned if the headman stopped snoring. There was much more of this and the talk went on and on, and though Biria felt she was doing most of the work, she loved it all.

It was very beautiful in that place, and there was a fragrance from the ginger lily and the strong heady smell of tropic earth, and something salty from the sea beyond. When the taro was cooked Biria set it out and began to eat. She ate a good meal, for they planned a long night of fishing, but Ingat was still talking, and she ate almost nothing, picking at the roots only and not doing more than taste them.

Biria finished the cooked taro, for she was a woman who hated waste, and then they were about to set out when Ingat had a new idea.

"Carry me," she said. "Carry me on your shoulders like a picaninny." And Biria smiled, and Ingat climbed upon her shoulders and rode along the path.

Biria felt she was being foolish. She was a woman too old, she thought, for this kind of play; but as she went along she had the strange feeling that she was carrying her own child. She was happy in carrying Ingat. In a little while she took the cigarette from her mouth and passed it up to Ingat as mothers among her people have shared tobacco with their babies since time began. When Ingat played the naughty child and did not give it back Biria chuckled to herself and did not feel resentful.

"I am a fool," she thought, but she was not any the less happy.

And now Ingat had found the frogs in the billum net, and she began to eat them, and still Biria was happy, though Ingat could quite well have stayed her stomach earlier with the taro. But in the silence when Ingat was eating, Biria, trotting along the bush track with Ingat on her shoulders, heard again the thin sound of the sing-sing rising and falling on the evening air, for now it was very dark. She heard it; or she thought she heard it; she was not sure which.

And suddenly a new thought came to her that shocked the deeps of her mind; for she remembered how she had reckoned Ingat dead while she waited at the junction of the paths.

"This is no Ingat but a devil-woman," she thought. "Ingat is dead and a devil is using her body." And she had very great fear.

For it was a terrible thought. It was something beyond her consciousness and her experience, but Biria was a brave woman and she showed no sign. But she felt sure that the woman on her shoulders was a devil-woman, and she counted up the evidence:

The woman had eaten no taro, but only picked at it.

She had ridden on Biria's back and she had made it seem to Biria that she carried her own child.

She had taken Biria's cigarette and the frogs for Biria's family, and Biria had felt no resentment.

She had not heard the music of the sing-sing that Biria could hear, but had talked of other things.

Biria was sure now that this was a devil-woman who was luring her on through the deeper parts of the forest.

Before they could reach the sea they had to negotiate a thickness of trees that, for some forgotten reason, held a bad reputation. When Biria remembered that too, she stopped and said, "Let's rest a while." She set Ingat down, or she set down the devil-woman that was Ingat, and then she made a little fire.

"We're making a fire already?" Ingat asked in surprise, and Biria answered, "I want to make bom-boms to light us through the black bush ahead."

Ingat laughed and sat herself down at the fire. So Biria brought palm fronds and made herself a torch.

She said, "While I have the torch I'll catch a couple of frogs to make up for the ones you ate. I promised Baisa to bring him a frog, for he loves them very much."

And Ingat answered, "We have the whole night, and there will be some time before the moon is up and we are ready to bom-bom the fish." She threw a little piece of wood on the fire and began to sing a happy little song to herself.

Biria took the torch and went up above the track and there she tied the torch upright above a little swampy place, with a vine to hold it to a tree-stump. The place she chose caught the little breezes, and the torch swayed a fraction on its base, and the flame glowed and diminished and its light ebbed and swelled, so that Ingat, who could not see the torch, could nevertheless see the reflections of its light, and would believe Biria to be catching frogs.

But Biria was running, fleet and fast as a cassowary, running along the forest track as she had never run in her life, her unfettered breasts thudding against her chest, her thighs heedless of the little obstructions in her way. She ran and she ran until she came to her own village of Labu.

All of the people were in the village and she told them her story. She told them that Ingat, the lively one, the little Ingat, the beloved Ingat was dead, and that a devil-woman had taken her body. She told them that Ingat's village was wailing for her death, while Ingat's body walked the forest tracks. She told them how the devil-woman had tried to deceive her, to lure her into the dark thickness of bush on the way to the sea; how the devil-woman had used her and worked on her to make use of her in some unholy scheme.

Now Biria was not a woman given to imaginings. She was a housewife as dull of wit as any; and though her influence was not great, the tidings she brought were alarming. For there was little doubt but that the devil-woman, having marked Biria for her own, would come to claim her.

So the men of the village went to work. They built a huge fire and stacked it with the cooking-stones they used to heat the ovens. And across the path leading to the village from the beach they dug a pit, deep and wide; and set men with bows guarding the path. They did all this with frantic haste, and when the stones were hot they took some and put them in the bottom of the pit and covered over the pit with a lacework of feeble sticks, and thus hid all their preparations beneath a cover of earth, very hastily fashioned, but nevertheless quite capable of deceiving an unwary eye. And then they waited, and heaped more wood on the fires, and set more bowmen round the path.

Now Ingat, while this had been going on, was sleepy by the fire. She waited a long time, singing a little song to herself. Once or twice she looked up and saw the torchlight glowing, ebbing and increasing among the trees, and she wished that Biria had not left her, for she was a woman who much liked company. By and by the vine holding the torch burned through, and the flame fell on the swampy mud beneath and was extinguished, and still Ingat waited by the fire for Biria to return, for she was a lazy woman.

A long time went by, and there was still no Biria, nor could Ingat hear any sign of her among the trees above the path. She called to her, and the forest was immediately silent, but still Biria did not reply. Ingat called and called. Then she made herself a torch of palm fronds and went to find her friend.

She searched a long time in the dark bush, but she found nothing, and all the time a fear grew on her, and her thoughts that were so happy became dark, and she was frightened. She came back to the fire and saw Biria's billum, with the spare lap-lap for swimming, and her lime-gourd for the chewing betel, and her awls and her needles, and all the little things with which a woman would not willingly part. She took the billum in her hand and went back along the path to seek her friend, or to tell others that she had gone. She was little and bewildered, and she was caught with a dread of the night's events.

At the junction of the paths she hesitated, but her duty to Biria was clear, and she took the road that led to Labu.

Behind her the dark pursued, and the night that had at a stroke become so full of mystery, so empty of a friend; and when she was just a little way along the path she began to run, and fear ran behind her, and panic caught up with her, and she cried out, a fearsome lost cry that was of that night of fear; and so, running madly, she came upon the village of Labu, and the bowmen loosed their arrows, and in the same moment she fell into the pit upon the hot stones and was no more.

All the people of Labu came and piled the cooking

stones from the fire upon her little body that was so light, so proper a vessel for her happiness; and she was baked like a pig in the oven until there was little left of her. In the morning the villagers of Labu took that little and buried it in a grave a long way from the village, and they planted bamboos on the grave. Only then were they satisfied, and they said, "The devil-woman is no more. She is dead truly."

Each man told the story of what they had seen. Englaf, an old man, said, "When she burst from the bush her face was full of hatred, and her belly was hot with anger against us all. And truly, if the woman Biria had not been wise, last night might have seen the end of everyone here."

"Truly her belly was hot against us all," they agreed; and they talked a great deal about the night, though there was little more they could say. And for the first time in her life, for she was a silent woman, Biria talked more than anyone.

"Her eyes flashed with hatred, and her mouth worked with anger, and she screamed at us all," she said. "But most of all her hatred was for me, this devil-woman. She hated me most because I tricked her with the torch to gain time for us, out there in the bush. And truly I was close to Death. I carried Death on my shoulders like a child."

But once, sitting quietly, she said, "It is sad about Ingat, for she was a happy woman and I was her friend. My heart was always turned to her. I was fond of her, and I used to do whatever she asked of me. It is sad about her. I will never have another friend like her."

THE HONEYSUCKLE TRAP
Barbara Ker Wilson

The Carringtons "collect islands". That's the way they describe it. For several years now they have chosen to spend holidays on various islands—the Hebrides, the Isles of Scilly, and, farther across the sea, Majorca, Corsica, and Sicily. One year they went as far as Rhodes. From all these expeditions they bring home to London amusing tales of their experiences, gossip about the people they've met, colour slides of land- and seascapes, as well as objects, things—Mary Carrington would never refer to them as mementoes, still less as souvenirs—to remind them of the places they've seen. A silver brooch from Skye which Mary often wears; a painted plate from Majorca which they use at their wine-and-cheese parties; terra-cotta pots from Greece that Peter has hung on the walls of their courtyard garden, trailing decorative ivy. They're a pleasant couple; young, good company, both practical by nature. Each a little unimaginative, perhaps—at least, that's what I used to think. Now, I'm not so sure.

When they returned home last month from their latest holiday, they asked me to visit them. I expected the usual post-holiday gathering of their friends, the wine and cheese, the colour slides slotting into position one after another, with Peter's lighthearted commentary and additional remarks thrown in by Mary from time to time. You know the sort of thing. I was to be surprised.

162

I decided to walk to their house. They live in Chelsea, not far from my flat. It was a fine evening in late summer, and part of my way lay beside the river. I enjoy walking beside the Thames at dusk; that night the sunset seemed to reproduce a Turner painting. St Paul's was silhouetted against the bloodshot sky—a similar effect, I thought, to the way it must have looked during the Blitz. But, as always, I firmly turned away my thoughts from the wartime years. I do not care to dwell on them.

Possibly it is hindsight to say now that I felt some premonition that the evening was to bring the strangest experience of my life—I don't think *that* is an exaggeration. Maybe it was only the dusk, the river and the sunset: a powerful enough combination, surely.

When I got to the Carringtons' house, I wondered if I had mistaken the time, or the day. There were no cars parked outside. Clearly, however, I was expected. Mary greeted me warmly.

"We've not asked anyone else," she said. "We decided we'd like to have you all to ourselves, Edward."

Did I discern a slightly—defensive—note in her voice?

"That sounds rather as though you intend to serve me up as an entrée," I remarked, smiling. It was the sort of facetious remark I often found myself making in the Carringtons' company. Yet their company was always pleasant.

Strangely, there seemed to be a time-lag in Mary's responsive smile. Why, I wondered? It wasn't a very good joke, but then Mary's code of polite behaviour did not grade her response to jokes—they were automatically accorded a smile or a laugh.

Peter had just opened a bottle of whisky. He seemed the same as ever. "The usual duty-free loot," he said with a grin as he handed me my drink.

That was a Carrington post-holiday cliché. Don't, by the way, misunderstand me. I don't mean to jibe at the

Carringtons, or sneer at them. Not at all. It is good to have some friends of reliable temperament. I relax and bask in the warmth of their clichés, their predictable social behaviour. Which fact only made my experience that evening the more unusual.

As we sat down to eat—and it was really most pleasant to be given a delicious casserole for a change, instead of nibbling on Camembert or coping with an adhesive *fondue*; moreover, Peter's loot also comprised an extremely acceptable bottle of Burgundy—I could sense that Mary was longing to tell me something; it was almost as though I were sitting next to a child who had a confession to make. But I could sense, too, that she did not know how to begin her telling, her confession, whichever it was. Perhaps it was both.

"And how was the holiday?" I asked. Helpfully, I hoped. "Interesting? Good weather? Food tolerable?"

"Oh yes. The sun shone. Beautifully quiet and relaxing, just what we needed. Good swimming. We enjoyed the inn. One or two amusing people." Mary's somewhat stacatto reply was, in effect, the sort of message she'd scrawled on innumerable scenic postcards which I had received from various islands over a handful of summertimes. It sounded dismissive of my inquiry, as though such things as those I'd listed were not of real importance.

"You've added another island to your collection," I remarked. The odd thing was—I realized that while I was speaking their language, as it were (the habit I fell into, chameleon-like, whenever I crossed their threshold), this evening they, I felt sure, were trying, even with some measure of desperation, to make contact with me on a different level than our usual one. The immediate problem was, how were we to meet one another?

"Another island—yes," Peter said, in what for him was a remarkably serious tone of voice.

The choice, I recalled, had been Peter's that year. Some

months ago, they'd sought information from me about the island, wanting to know something of its history. I had bored them a little, I fear; when you are used to teaching history all day long, it is difficult not to relapse into a classroom attitude.

No, there is more to it than that. Much more. I must relate the whole experience properly. I had bored them deliberately; not from any unfriendly feeling, but to compensate—instinctively, I suppose—for the sudden surge of adrenalin through my veins when, here in this same room, those few months ago, Peter had said quite out of the blue: "Tell us about Sark, Edward."

Sark: The word, and his seeming—but, as I quickly realized quite unintentional—implication that something was known of a connection between the island and myself in past years, had the effect of a pistol pointed at my head. *A Luger automatic, held by a man in field-grey uniform* ... My meticulous wartime training had taken charge, immediately, even after all the years that had gone by. Hooding my eyes, I had expounded—pompous word—on the history of the Channel Islands, my boring monologue serving to mask the shock I had received. I remember likening the Channel Islands to stepping-stones lying between the coasts of France and England, England and France. I positively lectured the Carringtons, telling them how as stepping-stones the Islands had been used by French refugees escaping from religious persecution, so that many Huguenot family trees, transplanted, had flourished there; and, during the second world war, by Germany, who invaded the Islands in 1940 and occupied them until the end of the war—as the first stage, so it was thought, of Hitler's invasion of Britain. This is disputed as fact, yet, at the same time as the ports of north-west France were filled with German invasion troops ready to embark for England, sixty-one barges lay in the seas between Guernsey, Herm and Sark, ready to transport troops and equipment to

165

England, while Guernsey's airfield was filled with planes ready to escort the invaders. *I saw these things.*

"Tell us about Sark, Edward": it had, after all, only been Peter's way of revealing their latest choice of island for the annual holiday. They'd stayed at the inn on Little Sark, which is connected by a narrow causeway to the rest of the island.

"A picturesque old place—the inn, I mean," Mary said now, turning the stem of her wine-glass between her fingers as we sat at the table. "Lots of tales about smugglers—you know the sort of thing: laces for a lady, letters for a spy . . ."

And watch the wall, my darling, while the gentlemen go by. But I didn't finish the quotation aloud. I am squeamish about finishing off other people's quotations; it seems too much like jumping down their throats. Nor, this time, did I deduce any unfounded implication from Mary's particular choice of line. "Tell us about Sark, Edward": what an extraordinarily unfortuitous stringing together of five simple words that had been.

Well, the next moment, and on my part quite inadvertently, I returned shock for shock. "Any ghosts?" I asked.

The effect of my lighthearted query was, almost literally, shattering. Mary dropped her wine-glass; although it did not actually shatter, Burgundy ran over the polished tabletop like uncongealing blood.

"How did you *know*?" she gasped.

Peter, too, was staring at me. "We haven't told anyone else about it; you must be riding a thoughtwave, Edward."

I was astonished by their reaction; inevitably, too, my former training raised in me a faintly critical attitude in the face of such undisguised revelation of feeling. But at least, at last, we'd found our stepping-stone, our causeway for communication. I uprighted Mary's glass and then dispensed what wine remained in the bottle between the three of us. It seemed only natural at that point to assume Peter's rôle of host.

I sat back, cupping my wine-glass in both hands. "Tell me," I said.

Mary mopped at the spilled wine with her table napkin. Conversely, this action seemed to help her words to flow. "It was—oh, so strange, Edward. Yet all rather vague, really. You see, we decided to go for a walk one afternoon—"

"One does, in Sark," Peter broke in. He had collected his thoughts, momentarily scattered as the wine was spilled. "No vehicles have ever been allowed on the island, as you probably know. Only the farm tractors—otherwise it's horse-and-buggy, and bicycle."

I could, if I'd wished, have corrected him on a technical point there. During the Nazi occupation, the ban on cars, lorries and motor-cycles had been broken for the first and only time. *How strange it had been to hear the revving of engines; how the vehicles had stirred the dusty roads.*

Mary resumed the story. "We set off after lunch. It was a lovely day, sunny with a slight breeze—just right for walking. We crossed the causeway and set off right across the island, heading for Dixcart Bay."

Involuntarily my senses became alert as I heard that name, but I am sure they noticed nothing.

"Everything seemed airy and clean—the sea sparkled and the seagulls looked extra white, like television ads for some detergent." Mary laughed softly. "We took great gulps of sea air and felt madly healthy and energetic. It took us— oh, a couple of hours to reach the far end of the island, and then we thought we'd look for a place to have some afternoon tea. We couldn't find anywhere in the village, so we wandered on quite a way past the pub—it was shut, of course—and then we suddenly found ourselves walking in a narrow lane, completely overgrown with honeysuckle and dog-roses."

Here I closed my eyes for a second. This was

unbelievable. I could have spoken Mary's next words for her.

"It was like walking through a warm, sweet-smelling tunnel. The scent of honeysuckle was overpowering. I felt almost—choked—by it."

Peter smiled uneasily. "That lane really scared Mary. And do you know, Edward, it was quite silent. That was— eerie, I must admit. It was just as though all sound had been abruptly cut off. There were none of the usual hedgerow noises—you know, birdsong, bees humming, that sort of thing. It was—stifling."

Choking. Stifling. They chose the right adjectives, these Carringtons. But silent? No. In my memory the lane was hideous with noise. I eased my collar with one finger. What else?

Mary's eyes were wide as she went up that lane again in her imagination. "At the end of the tunnel—the lane—we came upon the entrance to a big, old house. There were huge ornamental gates, rather in need of a lick of paint. They stood wide open, and there was a name on one of the posts: *Vieux Clos.* —There are lots of houses with French names there, you know."

I nodded. Yes, I knew. *The gates were freshly painted when I saw them. A military notice in German, French and English was attached to the iron scrollwork.*

Peter took up their tale. Clearly, the memory of that afternoon was just as vivid in his mind as Mary's. "The driveway—it was very neglected and overgrown—went between tall trees into the distance. You could just glimpse the house through the trees. I thought, we both thought, it might be a place where summer visitors stayed, and we might get our cup of tea there."

"It was still awfully quiet," Mary said. "Only our feet scuffling through long-fallen leaves and crunching over weedy gravel."

Leaves had been swept up, gravel weeded and raked, the

day I went to Vieux Clos. Slave-labourers imported from France were employed there as gardeners.

"We reached the house and wandered in," Peter went on. "The place was furnished, but everything was shabby and dusty; there was no one else around. We found a large room with lots of cane chairs and rattan tables, and sat down, but there was simply no sign of life at all."

"Our visions of lovely thirst-quenching tea and hot scones oozing butter and jam and cream completely evaporated into thin air." Mary attempted her more usual style of conversation. "Yet it was funny—we felt that there *were* people about, that at any moment not just one person, but lots of people might come rushing into the room. We didn't feel as though we were alone."

"Then," Peter said, "we realized that the room opened out, through glass doors at its far end, on to a long, covered veranda. And the strangest thing was—we both at the same time said exactly the same thing—"

And here Mary joined Peter in the exclamation they had made at that point: "Oh, *there* they are!"

"You see," Peter reiterated, "we had been expecting to see some people—we *knew* we were not alone."

"And—who were *they*?" I asked, hoping my voice did not sound unduly agitated.

"We had no idea, then," Peter said flatly. "We think we know now, because of what happened later. But all we knew at that moment was that we saw a number of young men dressed vaguely in the same way, grey trousers, open-necked shirts, playing ping-pong at tables set out along the veranda."

Ping-pong! That, surely, must be the last word one would expect to hear in a ghost story. The sound of that aptly alliterative yet basically frivolous word eased, for me, the tension that had been building up. I gave a short, involuntary laugh, as much from relief as for any other reason. "Ping-pong!" I repeated.

"Table-tennis, then, if you prefer it," Mary said almost crossly. "It really wasn't funny, Edward—it's the most extraordinary thing we ever—"

"I could hardly fail to realize what a deep impression the whole business has made on both of you," I said hastily. "Please go on."

"They were playing fast and furiously—aggressively, you might say," Peter said deliberately, "and we were only a few yards away from them, with shabby glass doors that surely could not be soundproof between us. Yet we heard nothing. They were obviously calling out to each other as they played, but we heard no voices. Their feet made no noise on the wooden floor. There was silence, absolute silence, as they hit the ball and it bounced and ricochetted across the table. It was like watching a silent film. And they—were completely oblivious of our presence. It was just as though we did not exist."

"We felt—like ghosts ourselves," Mary said, oddly.

I looked at her curiously. "Well, why not?" I said. "I suppose ghosts may belong to the future as well as to the past, for all we know."

"It was like that," Peter said. "Like being out of time. It wasn't frightening or creepy—at least, not at that moment. Just—strange."

"We decided to go," Mary said. "It wasn't until we'd nearly reached the gates at the beginning of the driveway that I remembered about the lane. Suddenly I felt—quite terrified. I just knew that something—that someone—was waiting in the lane."

Be calm, I told myself.

"I felt," Mary said, "as though to walk into that lane was to walk into a trap."

A trap. The honeysuckle trap. To lure two people into itself, as though it were some monstrous insectivorous plant grown vast beyond all imagining. I could not believe the strangeness of what these two young people were describing

170

to me. Its full impact had not really hit me until that moment. What eerie coincidence had led them to relive an experience that belonged to my past? I recalled a remark Peter had made earlier in the evening: "riding a thoughtwave". Could it be, perhaps, that my strong initial reaction to his first mention of Sark, those few months ago, had triggered off some supernatural association between our three minds? Or my suppression of that reaction, perhaps, in a poltergeistic manner? That might be more likely. I recalled that the frenzied actions of a poltergeist, the hurling of furniture, crockery, or lumps of coal, are often said to arise from a frustrated spirit trapped, perhaps, within a crippled body. I would never consciously reveal to anyone what happened to me one summer's day in Sark in 1941—yet perhaps my story had escaped from me in spite of myself, in some subconscious way I would never understand.

"We had to return along the lane," Peter said. "There was actually a wider road leading away from the house, but that would have taken us miles out of our way. I practically had to drag Mary into the lane! Oh, I wasn't indifferent to the atmosphere, either. I just wanted to get through it—to get away from the whole place as quickly as possible. To get the hell out of it."

"Get the hell out of it!"—Robson's voice, screaming down the lane, choked with blood, after the pistol shot. Blood streaming over stems of honeysuckle vines, over the creamy, waxen flowers. The sickening stench of blood.

Mary's voice sounded almost breathless now that she had reached the climax of the story. "We walked more and more quickly and then we ran. There was that stifling feeling again, the feeling we'd had the first time—"

At that moment, for all three of us, I think the well-remembered, sickly, cloying scent of honeysuckle actually seemed to pervade the air around us, above the dining-table where a few beads of red wine still lay on the polished

171

surface. Almost, I could tell, Mary got up to open the window wider. Almost I myself rose to do that.

"Then we were out—it was all over!" Mary said. "We came out into the open air and breathed freely and smelled the sea air. We were safe!"

"By this time the pub was open—we needed a drink," Peter went on. "And while we were drinking we got into conversation with the barman. We didn't say much, just told him we'd been up the road and into the big old house at the end of the lane. I think we'd even forgotten its name, for the moment. Then Mary asked him what it was being used for. We still weren't quite sure, you see—"

"He did a double-take," Mary said. "You could only call it that. '*Vieux Clos*?' he said. 'Been empty ever since the occupation, has that place. Been empty for years and years.' Then he told us that during the occupation it had in fact been the headquarters of the Gestapo. Young SS officers were billeted there, as well as their Commandant. One day there was a British Commando raid on Sark from England—apparently there were several such raids on the Channel Islands during the war, with the British seizing Nazi prisoners and information, and sabotaging communications."

I said nothing, but held her gaze as she continued.

"Anyway, on one raid, two Commandos apparently went up to *Vieux Clos* and took all the records they could find. Somehow the Commandant found out they were there. He went up to the house by the back way and waited for them to come out—he waited halfway down that lane, under the honeysuckle, and he shot one of the men as they were escaping, running down the lane just as we ran . . ."

"But the other man killed the Commandant," Peter said. "He—strangled him."

They stopped talking then. I replaced my wine-glass on the table, flexing my fingers. Did they expect me to comment on their story? I could find no words for that.

But they had given me more than enough to think about, if I chose. I thought of the ultimate cliché: food for thought.

"Edward, I'm so glad we've told someone. Of all our friends, you seemed the only one we could possibly tell. You're such—such a safe person, you see. And we knew you'd listen quietly, and not think it all too stupid for words."

"No," I said, "I don't think it stupid. Not at all."

Then Mary stretched out one hand to me—an unusual gesture. She is not a demonstrative person.

I took hold of her hand gently, cupping it between my two hands. Hands that could ... soothe.

"It's time you made coffee," I said.

Some other Knight titles you will enjoy:

SECRETS OF THE UNKNOWN

Since the dawn of civilisation, man has been surrounded by mysteries. As man developed, he managed to solve many things that at first appeared to have no rational explanation, but even now, in this age of super technology, there remain many things that just cannot be explained – or can they?
Some of the strange mysteries looked at in SECRETS OF THE UNKNOWN include: UFOs, Ghosts and Hauntings, the Loch Ness Monster, the Power of the Pyramids and the Triangle of Death. You can even test yourself to see whether *you* possess Psychic Powers . . .

THE NATURE DETECTIVE'S NOTEBOOK

Every season something new happens in the mysterious world of nature if only you can spot it. You can find out just what is going on by tracking down clues – like a detective – and by writing down your observations in a special notebook. You'll be amazed at what you can find at the end of a trail of footprints or under a hedge with a copy of THE NATURE DETECTIVE'S NOTEBOOK as your guide.

KNIGHT BOOKS

FLAMERS

Escape from the Planet of Death ...

Even as he watched – even before he had time to be afraid – Mykl saw the Gunship swallowed in flame, flooded in fire. But then a flamer tore through the leg of his ecosuit, and there were others close to him, flashing by him, and his helmet might be hit – He began to stagger back to the settlement, through hailstorms of fire. But he could not take his eyes off the Gunship. By now it was no longer its own shape. It had changed, horribly ...

PALE INVADERS

'Of course you're kept from knowing ... but one day you could understand ...'

Life was peaceful in the secluded valley where Gerald and Susan lived with the others. No danger threatened them. They did not know what had happened so long ago.

But one day Gerald found out. What he discovered made him very scared indeed. And then the pale strangers appeared in the valley, bringing with them the dark shadows of the past.

KNIGHT BOOKS

ALSO AVAILABLE FROM KNIGHT BOOKS

All these books are available at your local bookshop or newsagent, or can be ordered direct from the publisher. Just tick the titles you want and fill in the form below.

Prices and availability subject to change without notice.

KNIGHT BOOKS, P.O. Box 11, Falmouth, Cornwall.

Please send cheque or postal order, and allow the following for postage and packing:

U.K. – One book 22p plus 10p per copy for each additional book ordered, up to a maximum of 82p.

B.F.P.O. and EIRE – 22p for the first book plus 10p per copy for the next 6 books, thereafter 4p per book.

OTHER OVERSEAS CUSTOMERS – 30p for the first book and 10p per copy for each additional book.

Name ....

Address ....

....